BROODING REBEL
TO BABY DADDY

BROODING REBEL TO BABY DADDY

ALLY BLAKE

MILLS & BOON

First published in Great Britain 2020
by Mills & Boon, an imprint of HarperCollins*Publishers*
1 London Bridge Street, London, SE1 9GF

Large Print edition 2020

© 2020 Ally Blake

ISBN: 978-0-263-08520-4

MIX
Paper from
responsible sources
FSC™ C007454

This book is produced from independently certified
FSC™ paper to ensure responsible forest management. For
more information visit www.harpercollins.co.uk/green.

Printed and bound in Great Britain
by CPI Group (UK) Ltd, Croydon, CR0 4YY

To my bright, beautiful, bumptious babies and *their* baby daddy, for living with my distracted brain, boxes of books and weird working hours, and accepting that that's just me.

CHAPTER ONE

IT WAS CHILLY in the high-country town of Radiance, Victoria, the day Sable Sutton returned. A damp, grey wash coated the countryside like a filter, but the air was as sweet and sharp as a green apple on the verge of ripening.

It was about as different as it could be from the squinty Los Angeles sunshine and bone-dry Santa Ana winds Sable had left behind.

She shivered as she stood by the wonky front gate. Vintage men's jacket rolled at the cuffs, light silk shirt and ripped jeans doing little to keep out the icy air, as her gaze skipped over the veil of sodden autumn leaves covering the overgrown path leading to the shrouded house beyond.

The trees had grown in since she'd been away, crowding the pitched roof, the dark gables, the arched windows, making it look even more like the Gingerbread House the local kids had called it. Not only because of its fairy-tale appearance, but due to the witch they believed lived inside.

The witch being Mercy Sutton, Sable's own mother. Drier of herbs. Maker of potions. Scowler at children. Spurner of public displays of affection. Private ones too.

Sable flinched as her left butt cheek twitched, but it was *not* her mother, poking her with a metaphorical stick through the bars of her cage, demanding to know why she'd come back.

It was her phone buzzing in her jeans pocket. A long message from her agent, Nancy, promising work, soon. Photography jobs on the horizon after no doubt calling in every favour owed to give her pariah of a client a way back in. Only then did she ask where on earth Sable was. Though Nancy barely acknowledged there was a world outside New York, so Sable had no clue how to explain Radiance.

The stiletto heel of Sable's ankle boot scuffed the ground, the scrape unsettling a crow who lifted into the air with an offended *Ark!* and a flapping of wings. She watched it fly over the trees towards the neighbour's place.

The Thorne place.

Rafe Thorne.

Her heart twinged, the way it always had when

the boy next door winked into her subconscious. Though for someone whose emotions had always run close to the surface, she'd done a pretty fair job of shutting all that down over the years, the twinges *and* the winks.

No use musing over brooding eyes the colour of scorched earth, when they were on the other side of the planet. Same went for wild dark curls. Fingernails permanently stained from the hours spent under the bonnet of some broken-down car or another. Body tough, lean and wiry. Yellowed leaves shifting beneath heavy boots as he chopped wood. Sweat glistening on his strong arms. Brow furrowed in endearing concentration…

Sable blinked herself back to the present to find her heart not only twinging, but now skittering, and performing some pretty spectacular thumpity thumps.

For the wood chopping was the last true memory she had of Rafe—nineteen years old and smouldering—the day before she'd skipped town without saying goodbye.

She let out a hard, fast breath, and gave herself an all over body shake.

Her heart had been through the wringer of late and was not in any shape to twinge. Or skitter.

And *especially* thump. Besides, that was not why she'd come back to Radiance.

When a person's life unravelled, as swiftly, relentlessly, and mortifyingly publicly as Sable's had just done, once the dust settled it brought with it a sense of clarity.

Her epiphany? Her meteoric success as a photographer, the notoriety that came from dating someone even more well known than she, and the creature comforts that had come with all that had clouded things for a good while.

When it had all been stripped away, she'd been left to figure out who she was without those safety nets. What she wanted.

And what she wanted most hadn't changed. Not since she was a teenager, traipsing barefoot through the forest surrounding this small town, ancient camera in hand, mooning after the local bad boy, imagining a softly filtered version of what her life might one day look like.

Deep down, she wanted nothing more than to be someone's mother.

So here she was. Back in Radiance. The place she now saw as the crossroads of her life. Where, if she'd taken a left, instead of a right, things might have turned out very differently.

Too jet-lagged to face her mother, Sable turned

away from the Gingerbread House, and gripped the handle of her suitcase, dragging it over the bumpy cracks in the footpath, and made her way next door.

Only once the overgrown forest came to an abrupt end at her mother's fence line, she stopped so suddenly her suitcase bumped against the back of her boots.

"What on earth—?" The mist in the air all but swallowed her words.

For instead of overgrown grass, sad patches of dirt, tangles of blackberry bushes, husks of old cars and farm machinery, there lay acres of lush green grass, a few goats, a cow or two, and a plethora of happy chickens. For a second she wondered if her terrible sense of direction had failed her yet again, and the Thorne place had been over the other fence.

But no. There was the tree that had once shaded a darkly foreboding pile of wood in the shape of a house. Only now it draped over a gleaming Airstream caravan, shining like a silver dollar against the distant backdrop of the fiery poplar, maple, and liquid-amber-covered foothills leading up to the peak of Mount Splendour—more of a big hill, really—that overlooked the whole of Radiance.

She'd not expected life to have been put on hold when she'd left, but how had *this* not come up during one of Mercy's rare, uncomfortable phone calls? Something along the lines of, *Oh, and by the way, the Thorne house burned down/ fell down/was taken up by aliens.*

Then Sable spotted a window slowly closing at the side of the van. Meaning someone was home.

Twinge.

Was it Rafe's father, the fearsome Mr Thorne? Or could it be Rafe himself?

Skitter. Thump.

Was Rafe even *in* Radiance any more? Her mother's news reports were clearly lacking.

Only one way to find out.

Luggage bumping along behind her, Sable strode down the compacted dirt driveway, around the dam—its golden-brown water a reflection of the cloudy autumn sky—and up to the front door of the shiny Airstream.

She lifted a hand and knocked. Her heart thumping so hard she could now feel it in her throat.

After a few long moments, the door swung open, nearly hitting Sable in the nose. And a lanky dark-haired young woman blinked back at her.

For a snapshot in time Sable imagined it might be Rafe's girlfriend. Or wife. Even while her stomach rolled at the thought, like a ball of wool tumbling over the edge of a cliff, she reminded herself she'd been prepared for the possibility.

And that it didn't change anything. Not for her.

For it wasn't Rafe's heart she was after. Not that he'd ever look at her that way again after the way she'd left. As for her heart? Bruised, shaken, and shamed by recent events, it was in recovery and would be for some time.

The young woman's eyes rounded comically. "Sable Sutton? Oh, my gosh! It's you! It's really you!"

A heartbeat later, Sable's synapses came back online and she realised it was—

"Janie?"

Rafe's younger sister had been a little kid when Sable had left. Not even ten. Now a grown woman, she threw herself at Sable, wiry arms wrapping her up tight. Tighter than she'd been hugged in years. Which made her bruised and shaken heart cough and splutter, like an old engine trying—and failing—to catch.

Sable gently extricated herself from the hug.

"Look at *you*," said Janie, eyes skipping over Sable as if she thought she might disappear in a puff of smoke at any second. "Still the wild-haired wood elf I always thought you were, but with an edge. Yep, it's official. You're even more ridiculously cool in person than you are in your feeds!"

Sable somehow kept her next breaths even.

She'd prepared herself for the possibility that some locals might have found her online. It wouldn't have been all that hard. The photography contest she'd won, and the prize—a year in New York with a place to live, a guaranteed gallery show and a top agent—had been a big deal. But it was her move to LA after that was all said and done, her connection with a certain well-known TV chef, and the recent blistering disintegration of said connection that had made her life the stuff of social media heaven.

"Thank you," Sable managed. "But I've never been close to cool my entire life. And the social media stuff? My publicist—" *well, not hers, her ex's* "—put most of that together. Ninety-nine per cent of it isn't *really* real."

Ha! laughed her subconscious. If only *she'd* figured that out years ago.

"Do not deny me my fervour," said Janie. "You're the most famous thing ever to have come from this place. Apart from Carleen McGlinty, of course. But she's locally famous. And only during the Pumpkin Festival."

"Carleen. Isn't she the one who—?"

"Runs naked through town after imbibing too much pumpkin spice wine? The very one."

So, some things hadn't changed.

Janie followed Sable's not so surreptitious glance over her shoulder into the belly of the caravan, then gave her a look—direct and calculating—that was so very Rafe, Sable's heart tripped and tumbled so hard she winced.

Janie said, "So, it's *not* me you've come to see after all these years, fancy suitcase in hand. Big shock."

Sable glanced down at the hand now white-knuckling her luggage handle and released her fingers one by one. "Is he... *Is* Rafe around?"

Janie shook her head and Sable's heart dropped.

Till Janie seemed to soften, just a smidge, before saying, "He's in town, I think."

Sable's heart jumped. If she didn't get control over the thing, and soon, she was going to do herself a damage.

"I can call him," said Janie. "Let him know you've arrived—"

Sable reached out a staying hand. "Don't. Please."

"No? Then I take it my big brother has no clue you're back. How interesting. Do you think he'll be delighted? Or will he cut and run?" Janie clicked her fingers. "Right, no, that's your move."

Sable flinched.

She hadn't expected her return to be easy. But then neither should it be. The things that had come her way without effort had disintegrated just as swiftly.

Janie flapped a hand her way. "I'm just messing with you. I honestly have no clue how he'll react. But, oh, to be a fly on the wall!"

No flies would suit Sable best. Or witnesses of any kind.

Being a person of interest in LA was bizarre. Strangers butted into her conversations at lunch. Posted pictures of her walking, talking, eating. They direct messaged from the safety of their phones with questions, suggestions, professions of love and outright vitriol because to them she was a construct.

But being a person of interest in a small town was a different kind of hell. They talked about her right in front of her. About her mother, about Sable's ragged clothes, about her connection with the Thorne boy. It had been harder because they *did* know her.

Which was why—when all this was said and done—she'd find a place big enough to disappear, where nobody knew her name. Nobody knew her business. A place she could live freely, where any decisions she made would be hers alone.

"I'd better head home," Sable said.

After a beat, Janie looked at her suitcase and said, "So this was your first stop? Interesting. Very interesting. Don't be a stranger!" With that Janie gave her a wave before heading back indoors.

Leaving Sable to stare at the closed door.

Well, she'd just jumped the first hurdle of her return to Radiance without tripping and falling on her face, which after the past few months was a huge win.

Sable headed back up the dirt path. Her stiletto heels sinking into the packed dirt of the driveway. And for the first time since she'd stepped off the plane, Sable felt herself fully breathe out.

Rafe's backside hadn't even hit the stool at the counter when Bear—owner of The Coffee Shop on Laurel Avenue, Radiance's main street—said, "Did you hear the news around town?"

Rafe sat. Grabbed a napkin to wipe his already

clean hands, a habit built on years of living beneath the bonnet of a car. Ordered coffee. And waited for Bear to go on.

For there was no stopping the spread of news in Radiance, whether you wanted to or not.

Bear was big, bearded and gruff, like a Hollywood biker. His eyes gleamed as he slid a glossy long black and a small jug of milk over the counter and, in his rusty baritone, announced, "She's back."

Napkin balled up ready to toss into the bin behind the counter, Rafe's hand stilled mid-air. Only one person he knew of from around these parts who would garner that level of ominous expectation.

Rafe tossed the napkin into the bin, damned delighted it didn't miss. As if not appearing jarred meant he wasn't. To push the point home, he lifted off his seat, pilfered a doughnut from the glass case on the bench, put the lid back into place. Took a bite. Chewed slowly.

And said nothing.

Bear, looking fit to burst, boomed, "It's Sable freaking Sutton! You know—the Aussie photographer. Used to live around these parts, before my time. Dates what's-his-name—the ice-cool chef from that TV show. Though, hang on, that all went kaboom a couple of months back. Affairs…plural. Can't remember who strayed. Scandalous stuff though."

Rafe didn't as much as blink.

"Come on," Bear protested. "You know who I mean, right? Even if you're not a photography buff. Blonde? Wild-eyed? Bohemian beauty?"

Rafe poured in a dash of milk, cupped the black glass in his palms, took a long leisurely sip of the steaming hot brew and gave the guy nothing.

Bear muttered about the sincere lack of pop culture knowledge from the straight men in this town.

Leaving Rafe to brood over the fact he hadn't known she was back. A scent on the wind, a rustle of leaves, a ripple in the space-time continuum—surely something ought to have alerted him.

Unless enough time had passed that ripples, where she was concerned, were no longer his to feel.

Bear cleaned the froth spout on his big coffee maker as he said, "Trudy saw her get off the bus from Melbourne not two hours ago, dragging a big fancy suitcase behind her. Story goes, she was heading towards your place."

That had Rafe off the stool.

Janie was home.

Bear shot him a look that said, *Got ya.*

Rafe threw a ten-dollar note on the counter and gave in. "Towards her mother's place, you mean."

"Her mother?"

"Mercy."

Bear's eyebrows leapt. "You're kidding." He scratched his bearded chin. "So, is that how you and the younger Ms Sutton became a thing back in the day? 'Cause you lived next door?"

Rafe let a beat slink by. "Held onto that question pretty tight."

Bear had the grace to blush. "Wanted to give you the chance to tell your side of the story before believing everyone else's."

Rafe breathed. And reminded himself that he liked Bear. And the guy was relatively new in town. So, while Rafe's part in the Sable Sutton story was ancient history, to Bear—his friend—it was news.

Rafe ran a hand over the back of his neck. Then again. Harder. As if warming himself up for what he was about to say out loud. "Yes, she lived next door. Yes, we were a thing. She was seventeen when her photos got her a shot at an agent and a gallery show in New York. She went. The end."

Bear lifted his chin towards Rafe, mouth down-turned: the manly man's international sign for respect. "My ex was obsessed with her Broken Botanicals series—had these huge amazing prints of fallen trees, snapped stems, shredded leaves. Couldn't afford the originals. He'd die to know she was here."

Rafe wondered if Bear knew he was grinning at the vision of his ex dying.

Then Bear swished his black-and-white-checked apron aside and pulled his phone from the back pocket of his black jeans and held it out to Rafe. "Do you follow her?"

"Do I—?"

"Online. She's got quite the following for someone who doesn't post pictures of herself in a bikini. Or isn't a reality TV star."

Rafe kept his gaze on Bear's face, refusing to look. Until Bear's mouth kicked up in a knowing smile.

Fine, he'd look, then they could change the subject.

Rafe dropped his gaze to the phone.

And there she was. Sable Sutton. Staring right back at him.

Chin lifted, mouth slightly open, long hair, a hundred shades of blonde, a windswept halo around her face. The pose said, *Take one step closer and I'll burn you alive.*

Notions Rafe believed he'd long since buried, began to simmer and shift. Ripples, after all. He shut them down fast. Well practised. From a time when reacting had meant the difference between dinner or a beating.

"You okay?" said Bear.

"Course I'm okay," Rafe grumbled. "Just leave me out of the story the next time you tell it, okay?"

"Done," Bear promised, his voice deep, and deadly serious. A good guy. A good friend. And there had been a time, in this town, when Rafe hadn't had all that many of those. Having the last name Thorne meant having a target on your back. Not that Sable had ever cared about that. She'd only cared about him.

And then she was gone.

And now she was back.

And his head hurt.

Rafe rapped his knuckles on the counter as goodbye, then strolled out of the warm, hipster haven and into the chilly autumn day outside.

Sable. Despite his best efforts not to listen, her name whispered on the breeze. *Sable Sutton.*

Rafe glanced down Laurel Avenue, towards the outskirts of town. Not the showy bit, with the quaint shops, the faux vintage street lamps, the autumnal trees overhanging the neat footpaths, but the old section. Not that long ago—before the beautification tourist money had poured into the outskirts of the snow fields—people had been hanging on by their fingernails.

His phone chirped. A message from Janie, reading,

Hey bro, you'll never guess who's back!

He put his phone away. And when he next breathed in, he could taste it.

Change. A change was coming. And it had nothing to do with the weather.

He shoved his hands deep into the fleece-lined pockets of his coat, turned, and walked the opposite way.

Sable didn't bother to knock, for her mother's front door was open, letting the cold air seep inside. There was also no doorknob, just a hole where a doorknob should be.

Her place in LA—her *ex's* place—had dead-bolts, security cameras and an alarm. Not much help when the person doing you wrong was on the inside.

Sable lifted her heavy suitcase over the threshold and trundled down the dark hall.

She followed the sound of Bob Dylan to find her mother in the sunroom at the far end of the house, standing on an ancient wooden step stool, hanging bunches of vibrant, dried chillies upside-down by hooks on the ceiling.

"Mercy?"

Her mother's hands paused, before she looked over her shoulder. "Sable," Mercy drawled. "What on nature's green earth are you doing here?"

Missed you too, Mum.

"I'm back. For a visit," she added quickly, when her mother's eyes narrowed, making her crow's feet pop.

"Why?"

"You could at least try to look happy to see me."

"Of course, I am. I'm just surprised."

Right.

Mercy exhaled hard, wiping her hands in the length of her flowing skirt as she jumped down

from the stool. Then she padded up to Sable, feet
bare, ankle bracelets jangling, long auburn hair
streaked with silver floating behind her like a
fiery cloud.

She stopped a good metre away from her
daughter. No hugs. Not even a pat on the arm.
"Have you been next door?"

Round one, here we go. Sable nodded.

"Didn't take you long to go sniffing around
that place again."

The urge to duck her head was potent. It took
every bit of courage she had left to fight it. To
look her mother in the eye.

Sensitive as a kid, Sable had always tended towards conciliation. Avoiding eye contact, making herself appear smaller than she was, in the
effort not to make her mother sad. For she loved
her mum, as hard as Mercy made it to do so.

But when it had hit her, a few months back,
that she had fallen into the *exact* same pattern
in her relationship with her ex—not rocking the
boat, putting his needs, his career first—that had
been the real beginning of the end.

First time she'd stood up for herself, in a real
way, he'd acted swiftly, brutally unburdening
himself of all the secrets and lies she'd allowed

herself to simply not see in order to keep the peace.

She was not going to make her own needs appear smaller for someone else's sake ever again.

Sable lifted her chin a fraction. "I caught up with Janie. And kept any sniffing to a minimum."

Mercy snorted her response, then slanted her daughter a rare look of respect. Maybe this "standing her ground" thing would work on more levels than she'd imagined.

On that score... "What on earth happened to the old Thorne shack?"

Mercy's inner battle was written all over her face before she admitted, "He knocked it down."

"Mr Thorne?"

Mercy shook her head.

"Then who?" S*ay it,* Sable thought. *Say his name.*

"Rafe Thorne."

Never one name, always both. Like a serial killer.

"The father finally drank himself to death a few years back. Day after the funeral I woke up to a god-awful racket. Found your boy tearing the place apart. He carried every single piece of the place away until there was nothing left but the footprint. Then he dug that up with an excavator and grassed the lot over."

Oh. She hadn't even known Rafe's father had died, much less the rest. If she had, she *would* have sent word. Though which words? Sorry didn't seem quite right. Neither did good riddance.

"Why didn't you tell me?" Sable asked. "You know...when I rang and said, 'Anything exciting happen in town?'"

"It mustn't have seemed relevant at the time."

Relevant? Hang on... "Did you think I'd come running home if I knew?"

The glint in her mother's eyes said it all.

"I wouldn't have." *Probably.* "Just so you know. I wouldn't have run back. I had a life over there. Just like you always wanted for me."

Only, in the end, that life hadn't been for *her.* And Sable was more than ready to curate one that was.

"Anyway, it's been a very long couple of days. I'd love to crash, if it's okay."

Mercy waved a hand in the direction of the bedrooms. "There's a couch in one of the rooms. You might have to move a few things."

Super. Sable spun her suitcase over a knot in the floor before heading back down the hall.

One room was full of nothing but dust motes. Her mother was not a collector of things. Too hard to cut and run. In the front room her mother's unmade bed with its slew of hand-woven blankets showed through the wide-open door.

The only room left was Sable's old bedroom.

It was the first room she'd stayed in long enough to tack things on the walls: pictures torn from magazines, drawings, photos she'd shot as her interest in photography had taken off.

That room was why Radiance was the first place that had ever felt like home.

That room *and* the boy next door.

It took a nudge with her boot to encourage the door open as it caught on a rug that had not been there when she'd left. The desk under the window was a new addition too. And the faux suede couch with bottom-shaped dips in the seat cushions and an escaped spring in the back. In fact, not a single reminder of her had remained.

That was Mercy in a nutshell. Seeing sentimentality as a weakness. Leaving her daughter to feel as if she left pieces of herself behind every place they lived.

Sable sank into the couch with a groan and stared blankly at the bare walls long enough to make out the sun-stained echoes of the pictures that had been stuck there years before.

She imagined she knew how they felt.

CHAPTER TWO

SABLE WOKE WITH light burning into the backs of her eyelids. She didn't even remember falling asleep.

Opening one eye, she found warm afternoon light streaming into the room, sharp, square and split into shades of white and gold, like something out of a Rembrandt painting.

Instinct had her reaching for her camera only to remember how long it had been since she'd held the thing. Long enough she hadn't been able to find it when she'd madly packed everything she could fit into a single suitcase and moved into a hotel.

The impulse to capture the view dissolved away.

She checked her phone to see the time, only to find another message from Nancy in New York.

When do I get you back? Soon, I hope! I've a jaunty little Greek magazine super-keen to hire you. Summer spread. Rugged location.

In Nancy language, "keen" meant Nancy was hounding them. As for "jaunty little Greek magazine", that was no doubt a far cry from her last gig with Italian *Vogue.* And light years from a show of her own.

She sent a quick message back.

Hey Nance. I'm alive. I'm fine. Off the grid for a bit. Taking a break from work. Talk soon.

Her phone rang immediately. She turned it on silent and slid it back onto the desk.

She listened to the sounds of the house. No music, meaning her mother was no longer home. And realised she was starving. Meaning she'd have to head into town. For her mother's fridge would contain little in the way of edible food.

She slid her boots back onto her feet and swapped her man's jacket for a faux fur coat. A *tad* over the top for downtown Radiance, but it had been a long time since she'd owned Ugg boots and flannel.

She checked the cupboard for a hat or scarf to cover the mess that was her hair only to find something else instead.

A vintage Kodak box Brownie—the first camera Sable had ever owned. Picked up at a yard sale when she was fourteen years old. A week before they'd arrived in Radiance.

She turned the camera over, ran fingertips over the leather casing.

She'd not taken photos of people back then, so much as old leaves piled up in their backyard, jasmine trailing over their broken fence, a flat tyre dumped in the pristine creek that ran behind their place.

Chaos and harmony. Death and rebirth. Themes that had helped her make sense of her nomadic reality had resonated with people far beyond the boundaries of their small town after entering a few online contests had brought her attention. Prizes. Money. Opportunities. Notoriety. And, ironically, a way out of the nomadic existence that had led to her interest in the first place.

She tilted the thing towards the window, around waist height, and looked down into the small viewfinder.

The first time she'd seen Rafe had been through that lens.

She'd been lying on the bank of the river, the camera to her eye, stones digging into her back, a hank of her long tatty hair floating in the water, trying to get the best angle on the crooked branches hanging overhead, when a face had suddenly blocked her view.

And a deep, male, teenaged voice had said, "What you lookin' at?"

Sable moved the camera a fraction, until the angles were sharp. She held her breath as she waited for the waft of the gauzy white curtain hanging from her old bedroom window to hit the right spot and...

Click.

She blinked, pulled the camera away from her eye. A quick check of the gauge showed her a small black number eight. She turned the crank over, watched the word *Kodak* appear, then the number nine.

"Huh." Would the film still be viable? Unlikely. Nevertheless, Sable slid the frayed rope attached to the camera around her neck, popped her phone case in her pocket, then headed out into the fray.

It must have rained while she dozed, the sky now a dome of pale grey cloud that refracted the weak light in such a way it made a person squint. Still, surrounded by towns with names such as Bright and Mount Beauty, it really was a pretty part of the world. And at its prettiest now, bolstered by the array of rich autumn colours.

Sable tucked her hands as deep as she could in the satin pockets of her coat. Her breath made white clouds in front of her as she walked. Her feet turned numb in boots made for form over function. Her belly rumbled.

When she spotted a sign that read The Coffee Shop she could have wept with relief.

She ducked inside, a small brass bell tinkling as the door sprang shut behind her. The place was warm and lovely. Retro black-and-white-tiled floor, recycled wooden bar, huge shiny coffee machine, ironic quotes hung in mismatched frames on the matt black walls—Radiance had gone hipster.

"Sable Sutton."

Sable spun to find a huge, bearded man grinning at her from behind the counter.

"I'm Bear," he said, banging a meaty paw against his puffed-out chest. "You don't know me. New in town. But I know who you are."

For a beat Sable felt that slight lift in her chest that came when people recognised her. Once upon a time it had felt like validation. For her work. Her tenacity. For the hard choices she'd made in order to make something of herself.

But nowadays she was far better known for

being "that famous chef's ex-girlfriend, the one he cheated on".

She looked to the door, regretting the fact she'd have to head back out into the cold, her stomach still empty.

When Bear called, "Sorry. That sounded creepy. Please stay. I make great coffee."

Sable turned to see a face screwed up with chagrin, and beyond the gruff exterior a pair of kind eyes.

She moved to the counter. Sat. Unhooked the strap of her old camera from around her neck to lay it on the bench.

"There we go. What'll it be?" asked Bear.

She glanced at the chalkboard, an order for cool, weak, green tea on the tip of her tongue. But the thing was, she didn't much like tea, green or otherwise. The chef had his own line of them, so that was what they'd drunk in public. Like so much of her life, it had been easier to go with the flow.

No more.

"Double espresso, please," she said. "Strong. Scorching hot."

"Dark, strong, hot," he repeated. "Just how I like my men."

He held out a fist, she gave it a bump in solidarity.

Bear grinned. "When I moved here, I imagined I'd find hordes of them. Strong silent types. All scarred and muscled from chopping wood all the time."

They both paused, as the coffee machine hissed and steamed, imaginations whirring.

"No luck?" Sable asked when all was quiet.

Bear slid her drink across the counter. "Well, I won't say I've had *no* luck…"

Sable smiled and found herself wondering if Rafe still fitted that bill. Or he might have a beer belly. Thinning hair.

She hoped he was content. Had tearing down his father's house exorcised the demons he'd carried with him as a kid? Or had the fire in his belly morphed into something darker?

Was he single? What if he had kids?

No. *No kids.* That she was sure of. It had been their one sticking point, the one thing they'd ever truly argued about. For him children would never be on the cards. Growing up the way he had—his mother deserting them, his father an angry drunk—having all but raised Janie on his own had devoured any desire on that score.

She'd cried into her pillow more than once,

knowing that choosing him would mean giving up her own dream to have a family. A very different family from the way she grew up.

Before she'd taken the decision off the table entirely by leaving.

Only now, with her newfound clarity, she'd figured out a way for them both to get what they wanted.

Bear leant his elbows on the counter, bringing his face near level with hers. "Fair warning," he said. "Now that we're proper friends I feel like I should tell you—people like to tell me things. As if I'm a hairdresser, taxi driver and priest combined. And you're the talk of the town."

Sable shifted on the stool. "And now that you've met me what will you tell them?"

"That my doughnuts are fresh and my coffee is the best in town."

"Thank you," she said, and meant it. For she believed him. And it had been some time since she'd felt as if she had someone on her side.

Then, right as she began to feel better about things, there came a rush of cold air from outside, right as the brass bell rang over the door.

Bear looked up, his smile appreciative. Flirtatious.

And by the way the hair on the back of her

neck stood on end Sable knew—someone dark, strong and hot had just walked through his door.

"Hey, Bear," an all too familiar voice rumbled behind her. "What's the big emerg—?"

Like a subtle shift in the air, a vibration that sang through her bones, Sable felt the moment Rafe saw her. Recognised her. Even before his words slammed to a halt.

Had *he* heard she was back? Or did he simply know the shape of her, the way she'd have recognised the shape of him anywhere?

Bear cleared his throat. Motioned to her with his eyes. Reminding her that wanting to be invisible and actually achieving it were two very different things.

Sable turned slowly on her stool. Her cheeks burning. Blood roaring behind her ears.

And she looked up to see Rafe Thorne—the boy next door, her first love, the man who held her future dreams in a simple yes—standing right in front of her for the first time in nearly a decade.

She'd prepared herself for this moment. Practising conversations with herself in the mirror in the bathroom on the plane. But seeing him, in the flesh, it all went out of the window.

For the boy she'd known was no more as he'd been honed into a man with fierce abandon.

She was powerless to stop herself—her eyes roved. Taking in the curl of his cowlick. The bumps of his knuckles. The solid strength of his throat. Hair still thick, still curled, still wild. Stubble covering a hard, tight jaw. Lips that had always made her knees go weak.

Dark chambray shirt, sleeves rolled to the elbows showcasing forearms laced with the kind of roping veins that made a girl swoon. Collar unironed, top button undone—no, missing, having fallen from its length of unspooled cotton. Jeans softened in places where they'd been made to work hardest—knees, pockets, zipper. Rugged brown boots with the toes scuffed, the laces fraying.

Twinge, skitter, thump.

Now that there was no longer a planet between them her heart went on a rampage behind her ribs.

In both hands he held a piece of…something. She couldn't tell what. But it was a habit he'd had, even as a kid. Picking flowers, or grass stalks, as he'd passed, knotting them, stripping them, folding them… Those ingenious hands of his always needed to be occupied.

The flash of familiar brought her consciousness back into her body. Until she could feel the stool beneath her backside. The uncomfortable heat in her cheeks. The tremble in her legs.

For this was why she'd come home.

Not to flee the disintegration of her old life. Not even to see Mercy.

She'd come home for Rafe.

To ask a favour of him she'd *never* consider asking of anyone else. A favour that would change her life.

For she planned to ask him to father her child.

Not to help her raise it, or even know it for that matter. She wanted nothing from him bar his DNA. Then he'd never have to see her again.

She slid from the stool, the clack of her heels on the tiled floor jarring in the heavy silence. "Rafe," she said. "Hello."

Rafe, on the other hand, didn't say a word. His eyes cavernous, the deep dark depths giving nothing away.

She hungrily searched his face for a way in. For anger. Hurt. Surprise. For pleasure. Something.

Anything but ambivalence. It was the one emotion she'd never been able to match.

Then Rafe's gaze lifted away from hers, caught

on the big man behind him, and he said, "You, I'll talk to later."

Then he turned on his boot and walked out of the door. The brass bell singing prettily before the door shut with a decisive snick.

What? Wait! No!

Words spluttered and puffed inside Sable's head.

Until Bear said, "Go! Go after him."

And as if she'd received a metaphorical shove in the back, Sable rushed forward, dragged the door open and hastened after Rafe.

Past the trees growing out of little garden squares in the concrete, and out onto the road, her boots slipping on the rain-slicked bitumen. Her coat swung heavily as she spun in a full circle. The avenue was vacant in both directions. Unless he was hiding behind one of the cars parked at an angle towards the shopfronts, he'd vanished.

She let her arms drop to her sides and sighed.

What did she expect, showing up out of nowhere the way she had? That there'd be enough water under the bridge. That time would have healed all wounds. And whatever other naff sayings she could pull out.

She should have planned this better. Worked

harder on the first words she'd say when she saw the guy again. Something more persuasive than a breathy, *Rafe. Hello.*

"Ugh!" Sable went to make the long walk home, to make a plan for a proper ambush, before she remembered she'd left her camera in The Coffee Shop.

She turned to head back inside only to catch a glimpse of blue out of the corner of her eye.

Rafe sat on a set of rusty stairs tucked into the alleyway between the café and Mike's Bikes next door. One boot on the ground, another on a step, head down as he toyed with whatever was in his hands.

Heart thumping like crazy, Sable headed down the alley. Her shoes scraped on the wet concrete and Rafe stilled, his nostrils flaring, before he tore the piece of grass he'd been playing with in half and tossed both pieces onto the ground.

Laying hands on his knees, he pressed himself to standing.

When his eyes met hers, there was no ambivalence, which was a relief. But he did *not* look happy to see her. He looked ready to walk. Again.

She swallowed, licked her dry lips, readying to

stop him. But his gaze followed the movement. Locking onto her mouth.

She'd been sure time would have numbed any latent attraction. Instead she felt sharp. Achy. Overly bright. As if she were standing barefoot on an iceberg, while looking into the sun.

Then his gaze lifted, his liquid dark eyes staring into hers.

Time seemed to stop, and stretch and dissolve, until she was simply Sable and he was simply Rafe.

For one brief, crisp moment she imagined just leaping right in.

Rafe, she saw herself saying, *I want a baby, and I want you to be the father.*

Then a muscle flickered beneath his eye, and she saw past the unblinking facade to the heaviness in his eyes. Yes, there was curiosity, but only on the other side of a great gaping crevasse of trauma.

Leaping in was not an option. There was too big a distance to bridge.

Unfortunately, time was not on her side. Not only did she plan to stay in Radiance for as short a time as humanly possible, her own body was against her. For it had decided to make baby-making a challenge. Which meant she had to get building that bridge and quick.

Sable levelled Rafe with a look. "*You*, I'll talk to later."

"Excuse me?"

He'd responded! Sure, it was gruff, but that was better than *not* responding.

"Back there, to Bear, you said, 'You, I'll talk to.' Making it clear you didn't want to talk to me. I know a diss when I hear one."

Rafe's dark eyes narrowed and Sable felt her heart thunder, hoping the risk of playing things loose and familiar would pay off. Would rekindle their old rapport quicker than not.

And *there*. A flicker behind the wall. A gleam.

Rafe slowly moved to lean against the brick wall, folding his arms across his broad chest and staring her down. "This is how you choose to go about the first conversation we have in years. By quibbling?"

"I did say hello, back there in the café, but you must not have heard me."

A twitch. At the corner of his eye. Good twitch? Or bad?

"Unbelievable," he mumbled, glancing away as he rubbed a hand over his mouth. But not before she caught the quiver of a smile.

Trying to ignore the way the drop in his voice sang through her bloodstream, Sable cocked her head. "Would you like me to start again? Talk about the weather perhaps? Like normal people?"

Normal people. It was a line they'd used often. A way of coping with how the locals looked sideways at their less than typical families—her "alternative" mother and his volatile father. One of the many threads that had connected them.

She saw the moment he remembered. The tightening at the corners of his eyes. The way his fingers gripped his forearms.

But then he seemed to let it go. To *decide* not to care.

He'd been good at that. While she wore her heart on her sleeve, every emotion written on her face, he was better at hiding his thoughts than anyone she'd ever known.

A tactic to survive his father.

Just as making herself smaller had been her way of surviving her mother. *Had.* Past tense.

She lifted her chest, and her chin. Ready to show him just how big she could now be.

When he surprised her, saying, "I'd like to see you try to be normal."

And before she even felt it coming, she coughed out a laugh. Then gave him a look that said, *Re-*

ally. Felt a little tingly in the belly region when he gave her a slow nod.

Riding the rapport, she wiggled her fingers, shook her head, took a deep breath, plastered a big fake smile on her face and said, "Rafe! Oh, my gosh. It's been years. It's *so* good to see you. How have you been? Great, I hope! You look…" *Hot. Savage. Mouth-watering.* "Well."

Her words, full of faux cheer, seemed to bounce around the alley before dissipating in a hiss of steam as they reached his dark, still self.

Then the edge of his mouth kicked up at one side. She felt it deep inside. Attraction. History. Heat. Pulsing through her like a fresh current.

"I've been just…fine. Thanks." Infinitesimal pause before the "fine". Then he said, "You also look…well." The pause before the "well" was longer still.

Now what? Small talk? Big talk? Hard talk? Dirty talk? *The* talk?

Slow down, kiddo. Bridge-building, she told herself. *This here is all about building that big old bridge that is going to get you what you want most in the world.*

She took a small step towards him. "Bear told you to come to the café, didn't he? Just now."

After a beat he nodded.

"Because I was there," she said.

Another nod.

"And I thought he and I were friends."

A small frown, then, "Why are you here, Sable?"

Ah, the sixty-four-thousand-dollar question. One she absolutely planned to answer but not while there was so much tension in the air she felt as if she could levitate. "Look, can we go somewhere? Grab a coffee?"

No. Not a coffee. Other than The Coffee Shop, every other place in town would be filled with people who would gawp and gossip and she'd be in less of a position to talk, to *really* talk, than she was in this alley. And while Bear might promise to keep his lips zipped, she really didn't know the guy at all.

Before she could press again, the rumble of an engine—big, meaty, eight-cylinder—heralded a muscle car cruising up the main street. Neither of them said a word until it was gone.

"I have to get to work," said Rafe, lifting away from the wall, his arms unfolding, hands moving to slide thumbs into the front pockets of his jeans.

It was so reminiscent of the old Rafe, her Rafe, her chest ached.

"Right," she said, shaking her head. "Of course."

What kind of work? Should she ask? Or save it? For next time. For she'd make sure there was a next time. As many next times as it took till the right moment arose.

To ask him to father her baby. Then watch her walk away again.

It started to drizzle. Sable pulled the collar of her coat together.

Rafe stepped down onto the concrete and slowly walked past her. She had to look up to watch him pass. Catching his scent over that of the smattering of fine rain. Soap, diesel, and clean warm male.

Before she even knew what she was doing she closed her eyes and drank it in.

"You in town long?" he asked.

She opened her eyes to find him beside her. Close enough to touch.

"For now."

He gave her one last look, so dark and deep she had no hope of discerning what it held. And he said, "Then I guess I'll see you 'round."

She nodded. Then watched him amble down the alley and out onto the street.

The drizzle created a halo around the solar-powered street lights as they flickered to life as the afternoon gloom set in. Sparking off Rafe's dark hair, his strong shoulders, the water flicking off his boots.

"Hot damn," Sable swore beneath her breath.

"You said it, honey."

Sable spun towards the voice, hands raised, as her mother had taught her. *Men are dangerous. To body and soul. Protect yourself.* Only to find Bear coming out of the door by the steps on which Rafe had been sitting.

He had her camera and a huge rainbow-coloured umbrella, which he tipped over her head.

She tucked herself in beside him, even as she shot him a glare. "Were you listening that whole time?"

"Not the whole time." His expression was so innocent Sable had no choice but to laugh.

Then, "So how long *are* you sticking around? This time?"

Sable gave Bear a look. "Whose side are you on here?"

"No sides. All sides." He put big hands up in surrender before he slipped back inside his shop, leaving her with the umbrella.

When she looked back Rafe was leaning in the window of what looked like Old Man Phillips' rusty old Oldsmobile—only in the intervening years it seemed to have been given the fairy-god-mother treatment, painted sparkling blue with silver wings down the side.

Once Old Man Phillips drove off, Sable watched for another minute or two as the trad-ers of Laurel Avenue each popped their heads out of their shops to wave to Rafe. Back in her day they used to lock their doors when they saw him coming.

No pot belly, no bald patch. And he'd clearly made good. It was as bewildering as it was mes-merising.

Sure, to the very marrow of her bones, she would not get the same felicitous reaction, Sable pulled her collar up around her ears and began the long walk back home.

CHAPTER THREE

AFTER A LONG afternoon spent working beneath a Stingray at the Radiance Restorations workshop, Rafe opened the front door to the Airstream to find his sister in the small kitchen, headphones clamped over her ears, dancing as she stirred some kind of horrid-smelling goop.

He snuck up on her and jabbed her in the side.

Janie screamed, and spun on him with her ladle, painting the ceiling with an arc of home-made vegetable stock.

"What the heck, Rafe?" she said, tugging out her earbuds. "If that had been a knife—"

She stopped before another word came out. Her eyes widening. The colour leaving her cheeks. Not the first time a knife would have been brandished in threat by a Thorne. Though, thankfully, not by either of them.

And not in this space. This pristine, fully modernised, impossibly expensive tiny house of Janie's.

He'd had every intention of walking away from Radiance himself after knocking down his father's house. Letting the blackberries eat the lot alive. Till Janie—eleven years old, all knees and elbows—had looked at him and said, "But it's our home."

Next day he'd made a deal with Old Man Phillips to take the dilapidated Airstream off his hands, pimping the older man's Oldsmobile for free in exchange.

For Janie it had been therapy. Scrubbing, panel beating, building, surrounding herself with warm colours, soft fabrics. Comfort. A true home.

Leaving Rafe no choice but to make peace with the town. To stop slouching in the hopes no one would notice him, stop scowling the way they expected a kid of Ron Thorne's to scowl, stop refusing to make eye contact lest he see abhorrence in their eyes. To stop pining for the girl who'd left him in her dust. To become his own man.

Unthinkingly, Rafe took the ladle from Janie's hand and tasted the cooling mixture. He coughed as the tart taste hit the back of his throat.

"Give it." Janie grabbed the ladle right on back. "It's super healthy. And a work in progress. Besides, I had no idea you'd be back here for dinner."

Even while several years down the track, Rafe had built himself his own little sleepaway spot on the property, he often slept on the couch in Janie's van when he was in town. She liked playing hostess. Liked looking after him for a change.

And he let her. For while she was an adult now, which she was at pains to constantly remind him, the way she still bit her fingernails to the quick, and preferred staying in her little cave than being anywhere else, reminded him of all she'd had to overcome.

No matter how grown up she was, he'd always be her big brother.

"I thought you were flying to Sydney this arvo to give the final okay on the Pontiac," said Janie.

Rafe leaned his backside against the edge of the kitchen bench. "I was."

Janie glanced through the small window facing the overgrown forest blocking any view of the neighbour's house. "But you just had a sudden urge to stick around, hey? Did news get around I was making soup, or—"

"So you had a visitor," said Rafe, not bothering to pretend a certain someone wasn't forefront on both of their minds.

"I did! For about three minutes before she scuttled away. I recognised her in a second. All that ridiculously fabulous hair. And those eyes—like she could see straight through to my soul." Janie sighed. "I was smitten with her back then. Total girl crush."

"That so?"

"It was the way she moved, all slow blinks and liquid limbs. Like she was floating through life."

Floating through life. That was Sable. Like flotsam. Tossed about on her formidable mother's whims. Tossed to New York by a rare chance. To LA by some famous chef...

Now back again.

Rafe had no doubt she'd be tossed somewhere new soon enough.

As if she'd read his mind, Janie added, "She's different now, don't you think? Grittier, somehow. Grounded. Dare I say, more interesting?"

More interesting? Even as a teenager she'd been more interesting than he'd known what to do with. Sensitive, emotional, beguiling, and ingenuous, with those strange dreamy eyes, the kind you couldn't look at long for fear of falling in...

But that was then. And if she was "different" now, he was a new person entirely.

Rafe looked down at his hands. At the oil tattooed into the grooves. The bruises under half his nails. The stubby ends of his fingers. The swollen knuckles. Okay, so not entirely.

He felt the frown pulling at his forehead. He might still be found beneath the bonnet of a car, more often than not, but he was also a successful businessman. A well-regarded collector. Renowned the world over for his ability to spot a gem, to restore the unrestorable.

Not that she needed to know any of that. He did not owe her a thing. Not a conversation, not a coffee. Not any more.

Rafe tipped his chin. "You got all that in the three minutes in which you spoke?"

"Yep," said Janie with a grin. Then her eyes narrowed. "Hang on a second. She found you, didn't she? I can tell by the mulish look on your face. How was it? All hearts and flowers and swelling string section? Or did you pull a you and answer in monosyllables?"

Rafe shot Janie a flat stare, only to find she wasn't laughing at him. She looked concerned. But Janie had nothing to worry about. He leaned over, wrapped an arm about her neck and ruffled her messy hair.

"Hey! This do takes effort." She ducked out from under his loose grip. "Come on, I want to know how it all went down."

"While I want dinner. So, I'm gonna head back into town for a real meal."

Janie threw her ladle into the sink with a clang. "This is barely good enough for the chooks. Give me five minutes to wash up. I'll drive."

Rafe laughed before he even felt it coming. Janie, a Thorne and therefore a rebel, drove a tiny battery-operated tin can on wheels when he could have sourced her the coolest muscle car on the planet if she'd let him. "Funny girl."

"I know right. Don't leave without me."

Rafe smiled. "Never."

For Janie had been right. Radiance was home.

And though Sable Sutton was out there somewhere, and they might yet cross paths again, she would leave, and he'd stay, and that really was all that there was to say about that.

Rafe stood outside the front door of the Airstream, stretching his arms over his head as the weak wintry morning light poured over his bare arms and a sliver of belly beneath the lift of his old T-shirt, the crisp mountain air sending goosebumps in its wake.

The roar of a quad bike had woken him. Janie was out in the paddocks, zooming around checking on her animals.

Smiling, he turned to make his way back inside when he saw someone at the front gate.

Not just any someone. Sable Sutton. Sitting on a post. Boots kicking against the fence palings. What looked like her old camera swinging around her neck.

She must have seen him watching her, as the fence kicking stopped. She lifted her hand in a wave, hit the ground with both feet then started down the drive.

Equal parts disquieted and curious, he made to meet her halfway.

They came to a stop around two metres apart. Minimum safe distance.

She was carrying a tray from Bear's in one hand, the other she held up to her forehead as she squinted against the morning sun. Her shadowed gaze giving him a quick once-over. He figured he was decent enough in pyjama bottoms and a ragged T-shirt. Till he glanced up in time to see her swallow.

"What can I do for you, Sutton?" he asked, his voice a little rough.

"Me? I'm…" Her gaze dropped to his chest. "Aren't you frozen solid?"

"I run hot. Remember?"

With that one word, she stilled. Her gaze lifting to meet with his. The years stripping away. Then she shook her head, just the once, her hair floating and settling. Her jaw tightening.

"I brought coffee." She held one out to him, at arm's length. "Do you still take yours milky? Sweet?"

He slowly shook his head.

"Oh." She pulled the coffee back into her side, her expression flagging. Her bottom lip disappearing beneath her top teeth.

She'd never been any good at hiding her feelings. It used to terrify him how readily she entrusted all that vulnerability in his big, rough, dirty hands.

But that was then. This was now. And his hands weren't going near her vulnerability.

Since it was clear she wasn't going anywhere till she did what she had to do, he figured the best thing was to let her get there as fast as she could.

He held out a hand. "Just give me the coffee, all right?"

She looked up. Her bottom lip came free, glistening. Plump.

His solar plexus tightened. If he wasn't running hot before, he was now.

With a grunt, he stepped forward, tugged the

coffee out of her hand, then turned and walked back to the Airstream.

Sable fell into step beside him. Easy enough when he was barefoot and she in knee-high boots that hugged her calves as if she'd been sewn into them.

"I'm not going to shake you, am I, Sutton?" Rafe said.

"Nope."

"Because you have something to say."

"Yep."

"Then say it."

She opened her mouth. Closed it. Opened it. Closed it.

He might have enjoyed watching her squirm, if not for the tension gripping him as if his skin were three sizes too small. For while she was a pace to his right, he could feel her. The warmth of her. The peculiar, golden light of her.

"Fine," he said, his spare hand gripping the back of his neck. "I'll say it. I accept your apology. For leaving the way you did. In fact, I'll go so far as to thank you. Thank you for leaving."

She blinked at his bluntness. But he was on a roll now.

"You had an opportunity and you took it. You did what I'd never have had the foresight to do:

you saw beyond the hand we'd been dealt, and demanded more. I demanded more too, once you were gone. I demanded more of the town. Of myself. And it paid off. I have a good life now, Sutton. Janie too. So…thank you."

He stopped to take a breath. It was a heck of a lot more words than he was used to saying in one go. And as he breathed, something dark and dicey skittered behind Sable's eyes. Ghosts in her gaze.

Reminding him that this wasn't the naïve seventeen-year-old he'd once known.

He owed her nothing. And to be honest, she didn't owe him anything either. Things had ended, not in the most ideal way. But were endings ever ideal?

She was no more to him than a memory, now. No longer his responsibility. No longer his to protect.

"So, are we done?" he asked, no longer concerned if his words made dents. "Have you got what you came for? Because I really need to get on with my day."

She gripped her coffee hard. Her fingers long and lean, the nails almost blue.

Unprotected, a memory swarmed over him. Taking those cold hands in his, blowing warm air onto her palms, rubbing heat back into her fingertips, kissing the tips…

"This must be so strange for you," she said, snapping him back to the present. The feathers on her coat fluttering and settling, as if the ripples of her return now affected the very air around them. "My, just showing up, after all this time. And the last thing I want to do is seem obtuse. Or as if I don't appreciate how nice you're being."

Nice? If this was her version of nice, he wished he could come face to face with the jerk who'd skewed her opinion on that score.

But no. Again, she was no longer his to protect. Perhaps he ought to set an alarm on his phone. Repeat hourly. Till she was gone.

"Rafe," she said, taking a step closer, those vivid eyes flickering with more thoughts than he could possibly translate. "You want to know what I came for? Fair enough. What I want…"

She stopped. Glanced over his shoulder as the sound of the quad bike rolled up behind the caravan and shut down.

Knowing Janie, knowing how ripples messed with her composure, Rafe moved closer to the Airstream.

"I'm hungry," said Sable, matching his steps.

"Are you hungry? Of course you are. You were always hungry. Can we go get breakfast somewhere? My shout. Or at least let me get you a coffee you'll actually drink."

"I don't remember you being this pushy."

"That's the LA in me, baby. It's the quick and the dead."

A smile hooked unexpectedly at the corner of her mouth. He'd forgotten how it did that. First a dimple appearing in her right cheek, a lift at the right corner, then the rest followed. Like a sunrise.

Her beauty had been more subtle back then. *She'd* been more subtle. A little shy, a silent witness to life rather than the kind to dive right in. Deeply sensitive, which was what had made her such a great photographer. The ability to see richness where others saw nothing at all.

The kind of person you'd notice out of the corner of your eye. Till one day you realised they were no longer beside you, and the loss was like a crater in your gut.

Add a dash of confidence, a splash of experience, and honed edges and the effect was like a sledgehammer. A sledgehammer who wasn't going anywhere till she'd said her piece.

He took another step towards the Airstream. As did she.

"Wait here," said Rafe. "The alternative is you following me inside while I get dressed."

Her chest lifted and fell. Her throat worked so hard he was surprised she didn't pull a muscle. "I'll wait. Not moving from this spot."

Rafe jogged up the stairs. Nudged his way through the small galley kitchen to the smaller washroom. Listing, in his mind, all the things he'd already missed by sticking around even one extra day.

Three impending sales of completed vintage car refurbishments that he had to physically sign off on. Requests to eyeball several possible restoration commissions. Council paperwork for the local car show Janie helped him organise. He was known not only for his workmanship, but his professionalism. He did not let things get out of control.

So, coffee. A little food. He'd hear her out. Shake her hand. Make her think all was forgiven. And get on with his life.

For it was a fine life. Perfectly satisfying.

He imagined Janie rolling her eyes at such a comment. Her voice dripping in sarcasm: *Sounds like a dream come true.*

As a kid contentment hadn't even been in his vocabulary, much less his plans. As for authority? Respect? Success? Big words for better people.

But now he had them, and nothing was taking them away.

Rafe turned off the water, skin prickling with goosebumps. He grabbed one of the small floral towels Janie kept on the "guest" rail and ran it hard over his hair. Stopping when he thought he heard voices. Female voices.

Janie had found Sable. And let her inside.

"Dammit."

The Airstream was hardly guest friendly. It was compact, open plan. Meaning he either had to hide in the tiny washroom, till they gave up and went outside. Or he had to head out there, squeeze past them, to get to the clothes he'd forgotten to take into the bathroom.

Sydney, he reminded himself. *Ticking clock.*

So, he wrapped the towel around his hips— a Janie-sized towel, barely enough to cover his rear end—and went unto the breach.

At the sound of the door opening, both women looked up.

Janie, eyes the size of saucers, said, "Rafe. Wow. Um…you knew Sable was here, right?"

"I did. Thanks," he said, saying a hell of a lot more with *his* eyes. "Though she assured me she would stay outside."

"But it's freezing out there! Much more comfortable in here."

"Nice to know you're so concerned about everyone's comfort," said Rafe, lifting an eyebrow. Skin damp, hair dripping, he could feel his nipples puckering. The hairs on his legs standing on end.

Janie bit back a grin.

While Sable blinked at him. Once. Twice. And he felt the connection he'd been trying to pretend did not still exist twang, as if they were tied together with some invisible lasso that had just tightened around them.

"Janie," Rafe growled when the knot of the towel began to slip.

"Right." Janie moved to block Sable's view, to usher her back towards the door. "Come to think of it, that coat does look very warm. What's it made of? Crow?"

"Ah, nothing real," Sable stammered. "It's fake. Fluff. Stuff. But yep, definitely doing its job. Feeling pretty warm right now. And happy to wait outside."

Janie opened the door, and said, nice and loud,

"Sorry about that. He's not usually such an exhibitionist."

Sable's fading voice wafted to him as the door slowly swung closed. "Could have fooled me."

Sable didn't want to blink in case it rid her of the vision currently burned into the backs of her retinas. Acres of hard male chest. Naked. Rippling. That magical vee of muscle she'd only ever seen in underwear ads. And a happy trail leading beneath the edge of the minuscule towel held precariously at lean hips.

"Earth to Sable."

"Hmm?"

Janie watched her, head cocked to one side. "I was saying… Have you decided how long you're staying?"

"Staying?"

She wasn't *staying*. She was on a mission. For Rafe.

Not all the bits she'd just seen. Ogled more like. Other bits. A single healthy, hearty sperm would do her just fine. He'd never had any plans for them so he'd never miss it. Not that she'd put it quite that way.

"Sable?"

"Right. Staying. How long? Depends."

"On? Mercury's alignment with Mars?"

"Sure. Let's go with that."

Sable stamped her feet, the dew having seeped through the bottoms of boots that had not been made for the great outdoors. "What's he doing in there, do you think? Curling his hair? Sewing his clothes?"

Janie laughed. Then, in the same tone one might use to ask where they might go for breakfast, she said, "Just don't hurt him, okay?"

"I'm sorry?" said Sable, though she'd heard just fine.

"My big brother might never say so out loud, but he's really made something of himself since you left. He's respected. Settled. And a raging success. I'm sure you can imagine the amount of work he had to put in for all of that to come to pass."

Sable blinked. "I'm really glad to hear that."

"Mmm. The thing is, as a kind of cosmic payment for all the good that has come to pass, he has this thing about responsibility. About not turning his back on anyone. His staff, the towns-people, me. He takes that obligation *very* seriously. To a fault. Our very own St Jude, Patron Saint of—"

"Lost Causes," Sable finished.

Janie clicked her tongue and pointed at Sable. "That's the one."

Sable tried hard not to swallow. Not to let Janie know that every word felt like a barb, snagging on her vulnerable underbelly.

For a few months back she had felt like a lost cause. Humiliated, broken-hearted, and appalled at how she'd let herself become a passenger in her own life, she'd felt about as strong as a single strand of dandelion fluff.

But while she might look a little thrown together, and was deliberately vague in voicing her intentions, Sable was *not* lost. She was *exactly* where she was sure she was meant to be.

"Janie," she said, "I can assure you, the last thing I want to do is hurt anyone."

Janie cooed, "Gosh, look at those doe eyes of yours. So beseeching. So earnest. Just make sure you don't do it anyway." With that Janie jogged up the stairs and pulled the door open. "Come on, pretty boy! Your date is waiting!"

Rafe growled something from inside the van that sounded like *Not a date*. Then appeared in the doorway in dark jeans, slick dark boots, dark Henley, dark hair curling damply around his ears. Just big, and dark and so beautiful it hurt to look at him.

Sable might actually have sighed. Out loud.

"Yeah," Janie muttered. "This isn't going to end badly at all."

Rafe picked his sister up by the upper arms and deposited her inside the caravan. "Be good," he growled. Then he gave her a kiss on the cheek and closed the door in her face.

Janie's words skittering about inside her head, her feet cold and wet, her belly empty, Sable found herself caught in Rafe's tractor-beam gaze as he ambled down the steps.

"Hungry?" he asked, hands rubbing together.

"Mmm-hmm," she managed.

"As I remember it, you're buying. So, lead the way."

CHAPTER FOUR

BOTH BRANDISHING FRESH COFFEE—Sable's hot and dark, Rafe's cool and bitter—made by an exceedingly curious Bear, they found themselves strolling into Radiance Reserve, a series of parks bordered by dense forest at the far end of town.

Rafe took the outside of the path, his strides shortened so she could keep up, and Janie's "he has a thing about responsibility" speech niggled at the edge of Sable's brain.

She only hoped this expanded sense of responsibility of *his* didn't get in the way of her very good plan.

"So, this town, huh," she said. "A few interesting new faces about."

Rafe spared her a glance over the top of his coffee. Her throat came over all tight, her heart threatened to twinge. She told it to get a hold of itself.

"Bear, for instance," she went on. "Met him yesterday, love him already."

"You do know he's gay," Rafe said, sliding her a telling glance.

"Sure. Apparently, we have the same taste in coffee. And men."

She earned a double-eyebrow lift for that one. Then a chuckle, deep and rough and delicious. She'd forgotten quite how much she loved it when that serious face lit up.

"What's his story?" she asked, before clearing her throat.

"Rode into town a year or two back," said Rafe, "hoping my team could wield some magic on his favourite Harley: a 1974 Shovelhead."

"Your team?"

Another sideways glance, then, "Didn't Mercy tell you? I took over Stan's old garage a few years back. Renamed it. Expanded a little. Made a bit of a name for myself, bringing broken-down vintage cars and bikes back to life."

"Well, that's just fabulous! And no, Mercy did not tell me. Turns out she's very good at not telling me much at all. Such as the fact that your father passed away. I'm sorry, by the way. It must have been a rough time."

Eyes front, Rafe offered up a single chin lift by way of acknowledgement. And nothing more. Stoic as ever.

Mulling that over, she didn't realise where they were till they got there.

"Oh!" she said, her boots scraping to a halt as a pile of crunchy autumn leaves caught in a whirl of wind and swept across the cracked grey path. "I didn't remember this place being so close!"

Open during spring and summer, and during the autumnal Pumpkin Festival, Radiance boasted an old-style fairground named Wonderland Park. Complete with Ferris wheel, a carousel with the most amazingly detailed horses, and a hand-painted wooden Chair-O-Plane.

Not one for group events, or capitalism, or fun in general, Sable's mother had flat out refused to ever give her a cent to attend, so she'd watched from the sidelines, listening to the clatter of machinery and the squeals of joy, on many a balmy summer evening from a spot in the playground nearby.

In fact, the playground had to be close… Searching the gaps in the frail-branched bushes, she found it. There—the ancient rusty slippery slide, and wonky wooden swings—

"Our first kiss," said Rafe.

Sable jumped at his nearness, at the words he'd said, the rough edge to his voice. "What's that, now?"

He angled his chin towards the playground. "Over there. That's where we had our first kiss."

"No, it wasn't."

She remembered, vividly. It had been the night of her seventeenth birthday when she'd seduced him. If dragging him up to the loft in his father's barn, where she'd set out a dozen battery-operated candles around a picnic blanket, and pressing him against a tattered old hay bale and kissing him for all she was worth could be considered seduction.

She remembered being so impatient for her life to begin back then. So impatient for a future with Rafe. A future and a family. It had taken her a long while to truly believe Rafe when he said he would never have a family of his own. A while longer still before she'd left.

Rafe's gaze swung to hers. "Do you really not remember? It was a week before the park was due to reopen that spring. A bunch of us came down here. Jimmy Dale had snuck a six-pack from his dad's stash."

Sable blinked and just like that it all came back to her.

She'd been fifteen, perhaps. Rafe a couple of years older. Jimmy had taken a shine to her, invited her along with a bunch of senior kids to "hang out". She'd never have gone if Rafe hadn't mentioned he'd swing by.

There'd been beer. Someone had brought a guitar. They'd built a fire. Stupid, what with all the winter kindling littering the scrub.

She remembered wishing she could go home. Feeling angry with herself for not having a richer vein of rebellion. Why did she flutter and float on the whims of others? Couldn't she stand up and say what she wanted? What was she so afraid of?

Then Jimmy had dragged her from the swing and started to dance. Spinning and spinning her until she thought she might faint.

Till he'd spun her out to the end of his arm and let her go.

There'd been a moment of pure panic, when she'd been sure she'd trip, or fall, when her sense of balance would truly fail her, until a strong hand had taken her by the fingertips, curled her back in, gathered her close.

Rafe's hand. Calloused, and enveloping and so very warm.

They had been friends for a couple of years by that point. Best friends, really. He being her silent protector as she scoured the forest for junk to photograph, she his adoring acolyte, watching over him as he fixed radios, washing machines, cars.

And while he'd held her hand a million times, to help her navigate a path across a stream, carried her piggyback all the way home from the base of Mount Splendour the time when she'd twisted an ankle, they'd never been face to face, body to body, nose to nose.

Her hand on his chest, she'd felt the racket of his heart. His hand at her back had tightened, gathering her dress in his grip.

"Rafe?" she'd whispered. Bewildered, hopeful, on fire.

And then he'd kissed her. A light, sweet sweep of his lips over hers.

The catcalls had begun. Whistles and howls and laughter.

Not that Sable had cared. For Rafe had been kissing her. Kissing *her.* Till her muscles had melted and her insides had sung. Fulfilling the deepest, most secret wish she'd ever wished in a lifetime of wishes.

When Rafe had pulled back, he'd looked as glazed as she'd felt. Until a shutter had dropped over his face, as impenetrable as steel. "Was Jimmy watching?" he'd asked.

"Who?"

A small smile, then, "Jimmy Dale. The bloke who's been trying to paw at you all night."

She'd glanced sideways to see Jimmy watching her glumly. "He saw."

"Good. He'll leave you alone if he thinks you're with me."

"If he *thinks*— Are you *kidding* me?" Mortified, all the way to her very toes, she'd made to shove him away.

But Rafe had only held her tighter still. Warm and protective. Even then. "Stop fighting me," he'd ordered. "He's trouble, Sable."

"You're trouble."

Another crooked smile. Another arrow to her heart.

"The difference is, I'm only trouble for anyone who tries to mess with you. Don't you ever forget that. Okay?"

Feeling tingly from the kiss, achy from the knowledge Rafe had only kissed her to protect her, Sable had rolled her eyes. "Fine. Whatever."

From there the memory blurred at the edges, bleeding into a hundred other summer nights. A hundred other delicious kisses.

"I can't believe I'd forgotten," Sable murmured, her thumb tugging at her bottom lip.

Or more likely she'd blocked it out. A talent she'd inherited from her mother.

"Flattering," Rafe rumbled.

She shot him a look to find him leaning against the side of the slippery slide, watching her. Expression still guarded, but there was a little crack there now, a glint. Subtle as it was, she felt it. Like stepping out of the shade into a patch of sun.

"I got a black eye for my efforts," Rafe said.

Sable pulled a face. "You did not."

The hairs on the back of Sable's neck sprang to attention as Rafe pushed away from the slide, his moves slow. Measured. Focussed.

"After I saw you home," Rafe said, "waiting for you to shimmy through your bedroom window being one of my favourite pastimes, Jimmy and his mates came around. My father was home. So was Janie. He had her hold the money as he took bets. Took three of them to hold me down for Jimmy to get one good hit."

Sable's chest rose and fell. If Ron Thorne was still alive today, she'd give *him* a black eye. "Rafe..." she breathed.

But the telling tightness in his jaw took her back. When it came to his father Rafe had never wanted sympathy. Or help. She wondered how good it had felt to tear down the bastard's house.

"Hang on," she said. "I remember. I couldn't track you down for a few days. I thought you were avoiding me, because of the kiss. Then I refused to go to school, in case you showed up at home. When my mother found out I was skipping, she shrugged and went off to some herb festival in Yackandandah for three days."

Rafe's father had not been a nice man. But her mother's lack of warm and fuzzies had left their own marks too, like an old break that made itself known when the weather turned. She found it hard to trust when people seemed to like her. Constantly held her breath, waiting for them to snap.

Her ex-partner's therapist—the same one who'd told his client to come clean about his indiscretions, his lies, so that *he* might feel cleansed— had told The Chef that he believed Sable had "mother issues" that meant she deliberately put herself in situations that were doomed to fail. As if that excused The Chef's behaviour. As if she'd asked for his dishonesty.

As if she found it a secret thrill when those who professed to care for her spun her out to the ends of their fingertips…and simply let go.

Shivering, she tucked her cold hands into the warmth of her fluffy feathery coat.

Was that what she was doing here? Hoping Rafe might still be the one person she could count on to catch her before she spun completely out of reach?

No. It wasn't. This, coming here, was her way of catching herself.

"You okay?" Rafe asked.

She nodded.

Rafe tossed his empty coffee cup in a nearby recycling bin, and strolled away towards the fair-grounds, giving Sable a moment to collect her-self. To rev her engine. To focus.

She took a deep breath and looked up. Looked around her. Letting the uniquely wondrous land-scape of this place infuse her with the energy she needed. And it didn't disappoint.

Right now, the fairground looked like some-thing out of a Stephen King novel with the dor-mant contraptions looming over them beneath the low-slung pale blue sky. The Chair-O-Plane chairs drooping sadly. The horses' faces on the carousel pulled back in heightened emotion as if they'd been turned to stone mid gallop.

Sable didn't realise she had the box Brownie camera in hand until her finger slid over the shutter button. The pad rough beneath her finger-print. The box cumbersome as she shifted it to waist height.

Muscle memory coming to the fore, she set her feet a little wider, softened her shoulders, let the camera sink into her hand, then squinted to look down through the small viewfinder. She moved so that the spindles of the Ferris wheel peeked perfectly through a gap between a clump of orange leaves overhanging above and rows of evergreens in the distance.

She tilted the box a fraction, knowing it always shot high, took a breath, held it…

Then let the camera drop, till it caught on the cord around her neck.

She shook out trembling fingers. Blinked back into focus. And blew out a long slow breath through a small gap between her lips.

How long had it been since she'd taken a photograph because it called to her? Her reputation had led to commissions. Portraits. Fashion gigs. She'd been paid an obscene amount of money to shoot a famous rapper's dogs in an abandoned tyre yard. All of which was as far from those that had started her career as possible.

Her inspiration had waned correspondingly. Her ability to tap into her instincts disintegrating. Her confidence with it. She'd never been sure if it was age, waning talent, the different light, the lack of time, her lifestyle...

Or if she'd simply lacked her original muse.

Sable looked around to find Rafe over by the carousel. He'd hiked the sleeves of his black top to his elbows. Raked his dark hair off his face. He played with something he'd plucked along the way.

Sable's hands went to the camera once more. Gingerly at first, before the heft in her grip felt right. She nudged the focus until the vision was a blur of shadow and light. Then again until it was sharp, in her sights.

There was no zoom on the thing. The negatives huge. Perfect for taking poster-worthy shots. But she imagined Rafe's face in the distance. Such a good face. Strong. Serious. Achingly handsome.

Then he turned, looked dead into the lens.

Sable held her breath and...

Click.

She slowly let the camera drop. Her breath out a euphoric rush of air. When she looked up, the light, the edges of the vision, the reality beyond the iris, swarmed back into focus, like ink through water.

Rafe held his ground. Resting his elbows on

the fence. Watching her across the distance as she watched him. Surely it defied the laws of physics, the way electricity seemed to crackle and arc through the air between them.

Then Rafe blinked, frowned and reached for his phone. Answered. And Sable's next breath out shook.

The longer she left this, the more likely the hum between them would blur the lines. And she needed them to be crystal clear.

It was time.

She reminded herself, chances were he'd say no, right up front. Which was understandable. It was a huge ask.

But she had counter arguments. She had re-search. Doctor's reports showing the bare facts of the uphill battle she was facing fertility-wise. But also her general excellent health otherwise. Financial records. Photos of neighbourhoods with great schools and hands-on programmes and parks…

She was ready for this. She *needed* this.

"Can't make it happen if he's twenty metres away, kid," Sable muttered under her breath be-fore slinging the camera rope over the other shoulder, then making her way to the carousel.

"Right," said Rafe as she neared. "Leave it to

me. I'll see you in a bit." He hung up, slipped the phone into his back pocket.

"You have to go?"

"I do."

"Work?"

He nodded. Yet he didn't walk away.

She moved in beside him, mirrored his position leaning on the railing. Tried to appear nonchalant while her heart thundered and her palms began to sweat. And said, "Have you ever wondered what your life might have been like if I'd stayed?"

Rafe's entire body stilled. Big effort for a guy that tall. "Sable, I don't think this is smart—"

"No," she said, holding out a hand. "It's okay. In fact, it might be healthy to play out the disaster we would have become."

His face shifted, just enough to glance her way. All dark eyes, and suspicion. "Disaster?"

"Total disaster! Don't you think?"

His grunt didn't actually give away what he thought at all. But she went with it.

"I'll start. Okay, so you would have got a job with Stan. No doubt. You were always a magician with cars, and Stan was smart enough to see past the Thorne thing, even back then. While I would have probably ended up working at the Shop and Go."

Rafe winced, as she'd hoped he might.

"Taking photos on the side, of course. During summer, if it was still light when I got home. On weekends. Maybe branching out to photograph newborn babies. Family sessions. School photos. And that's if the townspeople let the witch's daughter anywhere near their kids."

Rafe was facing her fully now, slowly twisting and untwisting the long blade of grass over and around his fingers. "Sounds…dire."

"Right? So you're working, I'm working. We're earning a little money. Saving for a place. Or a holiday. A trip to Queensland maybe. But we're content. Because we have each other. So content we'd have been knocked up in a year. Probably had three in three years."

Oh, the ache in her chest as those words came out, so light, so blithe.

"So no holiday. No place of our own. I'd have had to stop work to look after the bubs. Which I'd have loved. Except we'd have had to move in with my mother." She let that thought sit for a good long moment. "How's that for a pretty picture?"

Sable glanced at Rafe to find his frown had

deepened. The curling grass had unfurled from his finger, and lifted on the light breeze. His gaze was faraway as he said, "No kids."

"Hmm?"

"No kids. The rest, maybe. But no kids. Not for me. You knew that."

The ache in her gut grew serrated edges. Even while it was *good* news that his determination not to raise a child of his own was still prevailing, the fact that he still felt that way, a man with his kindness, and goodness, and genes. He'd have been a great dad.

"Right," she said, shaking her head before she turned it into a nod. "That's right. So this, now, the way things worked out, your life is better, right? Janie's life is infinitely better. Just as it is."

He looked into the middle distance and said, "All true."

Had his voice trailed off a little there? No matter. Things were falling into place. Exactly as she'd hoped.

Till he said, "How about you?"

"Hmm? What now?"

"Is your life better now?"

She opened her mouth and closed it, trying to figure how to twist his question to get back on track. Instead she found herself comparing her mess of a life to her life back then: home fires and forest walks, creativity rushing through her veins, lazy afternoons spent with Rafe in the loft of the old barn. No, her life wasn't better, not right now. But it would be and *that* was the point.

He moved then, slowly turning to face her, his gaze intent. And he said, "I know a little. Of what happened. In LA."

"Oh?"

"I know that it's been more than a year since you've released any new work."

More than a year? Was that possible?

"And you and that famous chef of yours… you're done."

Hearing Rafe mention her ex was so unexpected, she flinched.

"Janie liked to keep tabs, kindly sprinkling me with news every now and then. Bear brought me up to date, when he heard you were in town. And fine, I might have searched the Internet on occasion."

A quick flush rising in his swarthy cheeks, he looked down. He tossed the blade of grass to the ground and leaned back on the railing. When he looked back at her again, his gaze was intense. Enough it made the backs of her knees tingle.

"If that's what this is all about, Sutton, if you've

come back here looking for a soft landing, looking for me to make you feel all better, I can't give you that. I won't."

Sable found herself caught in Rafe's dark eyes as he talked about "making it all better". A euphemism that set off a plethora of memories inside her head—warm, tender, knee-melting memories—as if they'd been waiting to be set free.

She had to physically shake herself back to reality. "That's not what I'm here for, Rafe. You can relax on that score, I promise. What I want..."

This was it. From here there was no turning back. She looked to Rafe, her past, present and future concertinaing till her throat tightened.

She fought past it, pressing her feet into the ground, firming up her foundations, as she said, "Rafe, I'm here because I want a baby."

Rafe's hand snapped back to his side as if burned. "You want—"

"A baby. *Your* baby."

Now the words were finally out she breathed deeper than she could remember breathing in years. Lungs filling and emptying. Spilling glorious oxygen through her body, her brain, until she felt strong, light and, oh, the blessed relief.

"I don't understand."

When Sable realised Rafe was physically backing away from her, she reached out and grabbed him by the hand. His warm, brown, strong and scarred hand. Held on tight. Using it to anchor her.

"Rafe. I was hoping—I *am* hoping—that you will agree to be my baby's father. Well, not *'father'*. Because I *do* know that kids are not in your life plan. It's what makes this plan so beautiful. I want you to be my donor. I'm not asking for you to sleep with me. There would be doctors—"

"To sleep with you?"

"No! To take care. Of your sperm."

He looked so pale, so stunned, it was almost funny. Though she knew that was the adrenaline making her feel giddy. She'd never been more serious in her life.

"It's all very safe. Clinical. And quick. Especially on your part. Once you…do your bit, that would be it. I wish for nothing more—no financial outlay, no physical help, no visitation. Nothing. No strings. Not a single one."

She was saying all the right things, all the things her research said might sway him, but she could tell she was making no headway.

Realising how tight she held on, she let him go. His hand whipped back, and he with it, putting even more space between them as he paced away from her.

Though he didn't bolt. That was something. Right?

"Rafe?"

His back remained facing her. He had one hand on his hip, the other in his hair. Tugging. As if he was trying to yank his thoughts to the surface.

Sable moved a little closer still. "I know you never wanted kids, Rafe. And I always understood why, even while I struggled to accept it. That's why we would never have made it. You and me."

She could have sworn she saw him flinch. But then he didn't move. He stood there. Breathing. Listening. His face turned just enough she could see his eyes were closed.

"Because it has been *my dream* since as far back as I can remember. No matter what else had changed in my life, that instinct, that *yearning*, has been a constant."

He moved a little then, his eyes opening. His face turning. His strong profile her focus as she said all the words she had to say.

"So why I'm asking this of you? And not some random donor? Or any other man I've met since?"

Something shifted deep behind the daze in his eyes. A flicker of discontent. An echo of possessiveness. It sent a shiver down her sides. She shook it off. Focussed.

"I considered," she went on. "Of course I did. I'm not here on a whim. My reasons for asking this huge thing of you are two-fold. Firstly, most importantly, you were so good to me, Rafe. I look back on that time with such fondness. Such gratitude. I would not be who I am if I had not had you in my life. But a baby, my baby—I've come to realise it's something I want to do on my own. No outside pressure from interested parties, no raising by committee. Just me and all the love that I plan to pour into my kid.

"It's all but fate for the women in my family to do this alone. My mother managed, in her own way. My grandmother too. I know I can take what they did right, and what I believe they could have done better, and I can do this well. This is my time, Rafe. It's now, or never."

Rafe's eyes grew dark, his body a study in stillness. Then he turned. Slowly. Face first, then torso, then feet.

His jaw was tight, his eyes dark and *apologetic*. He was going to tell her *no*.

"Sable—"

"Stop," she said, moving in to quickly slam a hand over his mouth. "Just…think about it. For a day. Or two. I know you owe me nothing, not a single thing. If anything, I owe you. So much. Yet here I am. Asking. Even while knowing I've set myself up for ridicule, censure, rejection."

Doom.

She closed her eyes, told her ex and his dodgy therapist to stay out of this. "It's that important to me, Rafe. So please, think about it. And, as a bonus, once all is said and done I will walk away, and this time you'll never have to lay eyes on me again."

His breath blew hot against her palm, and ripples of heat rolled over her skin like creeping vines.

Slowly, a finger at a time, Sable removed her hand from Rafe's mouth.

His nostrils flared as he licked his lips. His eyes drilling into hers.

And despite the intense emotion, she felt a curl of attraction so strong it nearly knocked her sideways.

Not now. Not *that*. There was no place for it here.

Ironically. For jumping him would be far easier than the rigours of fertility drugs, and risky timing, and the ache of implantation. She'd read all about it. Talked to people who'd been through it. Even joined a support group in LA when her doctor had given her diagnoses. Plural…

But falling into bed with Rafe would only make a mess of things. And she was *not* about to sabotage whatever slim chance she had.

The Chef's enabling therapist would be so proud.

Sable didn't breathe as the leaves skittered at their feet. Rustled in the trees above. As if even the wind was mirroring the restlessness surging through the both of them.

Then Rafe's phone rang, buzzing in his pocket a moment before the sound split the heavy silence. It rang again and Sable flinched.

"Answer it," she said.

Rafe slowly slid his phone from his pocket and answered, eyes not once leaving hers, as if afraid of what she might do if he didn't keep an eye on her. "Rafe Thorne."

Then, before he had the chance to ask her to wait, or tell her no, she walked away. As fast as she possibly could.

Rafe barely remembered getting off the phone with his Sydney team, and making it out of the park, for his brain was shooting sparks in every direction like a faulty firecracker.

A baby, he thought as he turned onto Laurel Avenue.

Sable wanted a *baby.* Not just any baby. *His* baby.

And it wasn't some euphemism for *How about we take up where we left off?*

That he *might* have been able to get behind. For the attraction between them was thrumming so loud it was hard to hear over it. Chemistry had never been their problem. Only everything else that was against them: youth, family, the whole town, timing…

A *baby.* His baby.

No strings. Not a single one.

Was she out of her mind? Possibly. She'd lived in LA for years. Who knew what weird foods she'd eaten. Or substances she'd taken.

He might even have grabbed onto that notion and left it at that, had it not been for the fact that he knew her so damn well. The only thing they'd ever openly argued about was her dream to be a mother and his vow to never be a father.

He remembered one such time—or maybe it was several memories merged into one— wrapped up in an old blanket in the loft of his dad's old barn, dust motes floating through the air, on the verge of sleep as her fingers traced the hairs on his chest, her soft voice going through the alphabet, listing possible names for their future children.

Annalissa with the blonde curls and obsession with kittens. Benjamin with the grumpy frown and kind heart. Carys who thought she could fly…

He'd never felt as torn as he did in those moments, soul-deep, right to his marrow. He'd been so deeply smitten with her, desperate to give her everything she could possibly hope for, but the thought of having a child to take care of made his head spin, his lungs squeeze to the size of raisins.

He'd had to tell her, time and time again, in the loudest voice he'd allow himself to use, to stop. That it was *never* going to happen. That he'd do anything for her, but he would never give her that.

For he'd still been a child himself, thirteen, and Janie no more than three, when his own mother had left, leaving the pair of them in the care of their father—a turbulent man who wasn't to be trusted with his own welfare, much less that of two children.

So Rafe had raised his little sister as there had been literally no one else to do so.

That first couple of years had been the hardest. Keeping her fed with no money. Keeping her safe when she'd had a tendency to run.

As she hadn't even been in school attending himself had been nearly impossible. They'd called him a truant, a brooding, troubled kid, when really he'd been doing his best, while his head had been constantly in seven different places at once. None of them good. How had his mother left them? What mood was his father in? Could he keep Janie alive?

But they'd made it, the two of them. A little rough around the edges, but thick as thieves. And while their lives were now solid, secure, safe, he had not forgotten a second of the hard work needed to make that happen. How sometimes even that wasn't enough. That bad things happened—kids got sick, authorities intervened, life got in the way.

He had no intention of going through that again.

All of which Sable knew better than anyone.

His heart twisted, like a wrung-out rag, as he tried to understand what on earth had made her think he'd even consider the idea of having a baby with her—

Not what she asked, his subconscious piped up.

Rafe rocked forward. Looked down at his feet to find they'd stopped. He scuffed a boot against the footpath, dirt and decaying autumn leaves shifting under his sole.

Seriously, though. To come back here, after cutting and running, not speaking to him in years, where the heck had she found the nerve to ask him to father her child—?

That's not what she asked.

What *had* she said, exactly?

That she'd found some kind of loophole? She didn't want him to *father* her child. Didn't want him to participate in the raising of the child at all. She wanted nothing from him bar his swimmers. Clinical. Safe. And quick. No support required, or wanted by the sound of it. And he'd never have to lay eyes on her—or presumably any offspring forged from the endeavour—again.

She'd left that bit till last. As if never having to see her again would be the clincher.

Rafe laughed out loud, the sound catching in his tight throat.

A day, he thought. *She's been home a day, and you can't stand still. Nor can you move forward.*

And now—because you didn't immediately say, hell, no, flat out, clear as day, unequivocal— she's out there, believing that you are actually thinking this ridiculous plan over.

And *why* hadn't he said no?

Because she'd tucked her hair behind one ear over and over again. She'd looked up at him, un-blinking, with those vivid eyes. She'd been so earnest, so hopeful, and so utterly *Sable* it had taken him back with a yank that had all but up-ended him.

Realising he'd stopped in the middle of the footpath again, Rafe rubbed a rough hand over his face, and told his feet to move. He grabbed a leather tie from around his wrist and pulled his hair back. Hard. Till the roots hurt. And made tracks to Radiance Restorations.

The scent of oil, the clang of steel on steel, the mutter of hushed voices, the tinny sound of Stan's filthy old radio playing country music from its place on the top shelf in the workshop ran over him like quieting hands. If any place could calm the tornado in his head, this was it.

For this was his home.

His father's old place had been a prison. The Airstream was Janie's happy cave. His Mel-bourne apartment, his London place, the hotels he stayed in when meeting clients around the world were simply places to sleep between jobs.

Work, endeavour, taking something broken and putting it back together better than it ever was—that was his happy place.

"Boss!" That was Fred McGlinty—tufts of sweaty red hair poking out of the edges of his grey on black Radiance Restorations cap as he ambled over.

Rafe nodded, not quite ready for words.

"Good, thanks," said Fred, oblivious. "Check this out."

Heading to a Charger up on blocks—only a polish and new tyres from completion—Fred popped the lid, slid behind the wheel, left the door open and gave the engine a rev.

It sounded great. Throaty and rough, but clean. A dream compared to all the other stuff in Rafe's head right now. "Again," he demanded.

Grinning, Fred revved and revved and revved.

And Rafe's twisted heart slowly but surely came down from the ledge.

Sable had meant something to him once. Strike that—she'd meant everything. Ensuring her happiness had been his number one goal in life. But the choices she'd made had changed all that. Irrevocably. She'd broken him when she'd left.

In a way his mother's leaving and his father's volatility never had. But he'd put himself back together—with determination, and guts, and by sticking to the choices *he'd* made in his life.

And while it was patently clear the attraction still hummed beneath the surface of every word they'd uttered, it was not, and never would be, the same.

He was no longer accountable for her dreams.

Ed, Fred's twin, poked his head over the engine. "Gorgeous, right?"

Utterly, he thought, then realised Ed was talking about the car.

The engine cut off. The guttural growl echoing in their ears for a few moments before the soft strains of Stan's radio once more took over.

A cough came from the corner of the garage, where Stan himself sat. All weathered skin, and bristling silver moustache. Local newspaper open on the small table before him. "You still in town, boy?"

"So it seems," Rafe said.

Stan closed the newspaper and shot him a glance. "Wouldn't have anything to do with Mercy Sutton's girl being back in town."

Rafe's fingers clutched into fists at his sides, nails digging into his palms. Hell, he couldn't even hear about her without feeling that *whump* of heat rush through him.

"Who?" Ed asked.

"Rafe's old flame," said Stan. "First car he ever worked on with me he was building for her. A hunk of junk VW Beetle they dragged out of the creek and called Rosebud. Or Periwinkle or some such thing. Whatever happened to that thing?"

Ed blinked. And Fred cleared his throat.

The muscle below Rafe's right eye jerked.

"Boys," said Rafe, his voice like sandpaper, "take an early lunch. Grab some petty cash and head to Bear's."

Fred and Ed didn't have to be asked twice; they left so fast they practically laid rubber. Leaving Rafe with Stan and Neil Diamond crooning in the background.

"You okay, boy?" said Stan, eyes narrowed his way. "You don't look yourself."

Rafe held his gaze and considered his answer.

Stan had seen Rafe through plenty. Had stood beside him at his father's funeral. Had sourced the jackhammer that had destroyed the foundations of his father's house.

A single man, like himself. Never married. No kids of his own. And content with how he'd lived his life. Stan had been a role model in the way his own father had never been.

But this? Sable's request? It felt too big. Too private. Even if he was unquestionably going to say no.

"I'm fine."

"Fine, you say," Stan grumbled., shaking his head. "Most dangerous word in the English language. Let me know if you need a hand?" He cocked his chin toward the cars that still needed tending. But Rafe knew the old man really meant he had two ears and would listen to anything Rafe had to get off his chest.

"Will do," said Rafe, then he made a beeline for the rusty old Road Runner languishing in the end bay, hitched his jeans, lay himself down on the tray and slid underneath.

In the shade and the cool, surrounded by metal and rust and oil and purpose, Rafe made his decision.

He'd find Sable, and tell her no.

And then he'd head off to Sydney quick smart. Without her nearby, the mud in his head would clear, the unrelenting work ethic that had ground to a halt the moment he'd seen her sitting in the café would swing back into overdrive, and he'd get back to living the perfectly *fine* life he'd been living before she'd swept back into town.

CHAPTER FIVE

SABLE MANAGED TO work her way through two more espressos at Bear's before he questioned why she was sitting in the window seat, watching the street as if it would disappear if she blinked.

"It's the only patch of sunlight in your joint," she returned.

He leaned in beside her, making a play at watching the street with her. "Sure you're not waiting for a certain brooding, dark-haired hunk to wander by?"

She glanced right, trying to remember the layout of the town.

"Wrong way. His place is that way," said Bear, pointing left.

"Oh, shush."

When her phone buzzed, an incoming call from her agent in New York, she shooed Bear away and this time jumped on the chance to answer. Only to find herself looking at the original Norman Rockwell painting that lived behind her agent's desk.

"Nancy?" Sable said.

"Sable, darling!" Nancy slid into view. "Is that really you?"

Sable waved a hand around her face to prove that it was she.

"Oh, my dear girl, how I missed that beautiful face! How's Hicksville?"

Bear shot Sable a look. Sable just shook her head. "*Radiance* is…overcast."

"Lovely. But not as lovely as Greece, I'm sure. That job is still yours if you want it!"

"Not the right time."

"Darling, it's always the right time for a paid trip to Greece."

"I am fine, Nancy. Really."

"Fine," Nancy scoffed. "The most loaded word in the English language."

Sable smiled. For there was no heat in Nancy's words. They'd known and adored one another too long for all that. Nancy had been gifted to Sable as a part of the international art prize that had taken her to the States in the first place. She'd been the only one in Sable's circle who'd never warmed to The Chef, despite the heightened profile he'd provided. The only one who'd stood by Sable when his truth had been exposed.

Nancy was more than owed a little sweetener. "What if I told you I found my old box Brownie camera in my mum's house?"

Nancy's mouth sprang open.

"With film in it."

Nancy's eyes narrowed. "Don't mess with me, kid."

"What if I also told you I'd taken a few photos on it too. Small town. Fall foliage. Hypernostalgic."

Nancy grabbed the edges of her monitor, her face filling the screen. "What's the name of that Nowhere Town, again? I'm coming to you. On the very next flight. So I can hug you. And steal that film and develop it myself."

"No, you're not. And I'm not letting you anywhere near my film."

Nancy sat back, grinning from ear to ear, her cosmetic procedures making sure the smile only went as far as her eyes. "Fine. If Nowhere Town is your way back to finding your spark, then you stay right there, for ever and ever if necessary."

"Oh, no. No, no, no." Sable glanced out of the window at the pretty oak-lined avenue right as a flurry of autumn leaves drifted daintily to the ground. Then a pair of little girls in tartan dresses and wintry tights skipped past, holding hands. "Not staying. Just…passing through."

"Stay as long as it takes, then. Call me any time you need a hit of culture. Or an accent other people can understand. Deal?"

"Deal," Sable said on a laugh. They said their goodbyes then both rang off.

And Sable's gaze went to the window once more.

It was a truly pretty town. All park benches and picture windows and overflowing flower pots on the footpath that were still there the next day.

Picturesque and patently photographable as it was, she couldn't stay. Not for much longer. She'd spent no more than ten minutes with her mother so far, and had already ground a layer off her back teeth.

Then there was Rafe, and her promise he'd never have to see her again.

Just thinking his name had her feeling warm tumbles in her belly and nervous jitters skipping over her skin. Needing to walk it off, Sable stood and slid her arms back into her big coat.

"You off?" Bear asked. "Need me to point the way to the nearest brooding, dark-haired hunk?"

She shot him a look. "No, thanks. I'm all good."

Besides, the longer she could leave Rafe to think over her proposal, the better. Meaning she had to keep herself busy lest she spy him, drop to her knees and beg. "I think I'll go check out the sights of the town. See what else has changed around here."

The sights included a hill that called itself a mountain, a thick twisty forest in which tourists often famously got lost, a closed fairground, and the few local shops she could see from Bear's front window, which was probably why the big guy snorted his response.

And yet, Sable kept herself busy. Checking out the ancient thrift store, the wool store, the sweet new community library, the cool bike shop.

Most people she met were friendly. Asking if it was cold outside. If they could help her find what she was looking for—and meaning it. But she also felt a few dark looks hit between her shoulder blades, saw a few locals whispering behind cupped hands.

She'd lived in Hell's Kitchen when she'd first moved to New York. Then spent a year photographing nature, finding life between sidewalk cracks in South Central LA. Small towns really did do hostility like nowhere else.

After a long, long day, jet lag now tugging at her eyelids, emotions having run the full gamut from euphoria to panic, once the sun set behind her, the half-moon casting a smoky dark blue tinge over the hills beyond, she dragged her feet towards the top end of town.

The shops had all closed. Radiance was tucking itself in for the evening.

As if her footsteps had set off some switch, the street lamps along Laurel Avenue flickered to life. Then a zillion fairy lights—strings of orange, strings of purple, twirled prettily around the trunks of the big old trees lining the avenue—sparkled against the inky backdrop of the twilight sky. It was beautiful. Magical. Oozing small-town charm.

Then, right as she wondered if she'd been going the wrong way, as her sense of direction was shocking, there it was. Radiance Restorations. And any feelings of magic, and ease, and charm dried up in a snap.

From memory Stan's old garage had been a third the size, an old wooden building with a single petrol pump out front. Now it had swallowed the plots either side, boasted a huge flat-fronted building, painted matt black, with several big silver roller doors, one of which stood open, and

an office door tacked on the side. Five gleaming, retro petrol pumps were lined up along the
far end of the neat block. With a handful of fab-
ulous-looking vintage muscle cars tucked along
the fence line.

The name of the business was displayed across
the entire top of the building, pressed tin in a
chunky vintage font, then again down the side
of each pump in fluorescent bulbs.

This was no small-town garage. It was the kind
of place that made reality TV show producers
salivate.

She moved in closer. Pale golden light spilled
from the only open garage door. Her heart skittered at the sounds of metal on metal. The shuf-
fle of wheels on concrete. The tinny sound of
an old radio.

She suddenly felt nauseous. As if the rest of her
life was hinged on the next few minutes. Which,
in all honesty, it was. For if Rafe said no, she had
no back-up plan.

She knew there *were* other options, of course.
That a refusal wasn't the end of the road.

But from the moment she first had the idea—
sitting in a booth in an old diner in Encino, dried
tears making her cheeks feel tight, deciding her
recent troubles weren't a loss so much as a gift,

giving her a chance to create the life she truly wanted—it had felt right. As if everything she'd done, everything she'd gone through, had always been leading her back here.

Sable took a deep breath and strode into the garage where she found the husk of an old muscle car with a pair of legs poking out from underneath.

And it took her back so hard, so fast, to the times she'd walked in on Rafe in the exact same position—body hidden under a car, left foot flat to the floor, right foot resting on a heel—she was overcome with flutters in her chest, tingles over her skin, the echo of a soul-deep yearning she'd felt every time she'd seen him.

The scrape of the old rubber wheels broke the silence as Rafe rolled himself out from under the car and Sable held her breath as his long, strong body appeared, an inch at a time.

His belt strained at his hips, his now dirty black Henley clung lovingly to the rises and dips of his broad torso. Most of his dark hair was held back off his face with a tie. His jaw hard, rough-hewn, with just enough abrasive shadow to make her fingers curl into her palms so as not to reach out and touch.

Rafe hauled himself to sitting, his shirt lifting

to reveal a hint of rigid stomach muscle, clenching as he moved. His eyes, when they met hers, were dark and full.

The air between them rippled with history and tension and things unsaid.

"Sable," he said, his voice deep. Ragged.

"Rafe," she managed. Then—because looking at him too long made her feel as if she might combust on the spot—she glanced around. "I can't believe how much this place has changed. Care to give me the grand tour?"

He wiped his hands on a dirty rag, pulled himself to standing and said, "There's cars. Tools. Spare parts. Front office. What you see is what you get."

She wished.

No. No, she didn't. She didn't want what she saw. She wanted…other bits, currently not in view. Nothing more.

She searched frantically for something else to draw her focus lest he see the heat flushing her cheeks. "So, what are you working on here?" she asked, motioning to the car.

With a huff of breath he lifted the bonnet to show a sleek, clean engine, light glinting off the gleaming metal.

She leaned in closer. Their shoulders were a

few inches apart but the hair on her arms stood on end, as if even they remembered what it felt like to be close to this man. "Tubes, wires, battery. Everything looks to be in the right place."

His voice was deeper, grudgingly playful, as he said, "You have no idea what you're looking at."

"Sure, I do. That's what those in the know call an engine. How many afternoons did I spend watching you fix cars? Years and years of afternoons before we became…a thing. I could probably strip this thing down and put it back together. If I wanted to."

She looked up to find him close. Really close. Those dark eyes of his were too shadowed to read, but the shift of his mouth she saw, its edge kicking up, just a notch, hitting her like a thunderclap.

Sable knew she should look away before she did something stupid, like reach up and run a thumb along the new line at the corner of his mouth. Or grab him by the shirt front and haul him in for a kiss. To break the insane tension. Or simply to remember what it felt like to be held.

And then she did something stupid anyway.

"Fine," she said. "I wasn't watching you fix cars. I was just watching you."

Rafe might have laughed it off. Or told her off for playing with fire. Instead—as if he was also done fighting the urge—his gaze dropped to her mouth.

Giving it the okay to run away from her.

"Something I've always wondered," she said, her voice only a mite above a whisper, "did you know I had a crush on you, all those years before I finally did something about it?"

His gaze slid back to hers. "Yeah," he rumbled, "I knew."

The heat in his eyes, no longer banked, no longer coiled, had her heartbeat singing, *Danger! Danger!*

"Even when you kissed me that night? At the playground?"

He breathed in. Breathed out. Nodded.

"And it still took us another two years after that to *actually* get together. Wow. That was some admirable restraint I showed."

"*You* showed?" he muttered.

But before she had the chance to respond, to push, he motioned for her to move back, and then he shut the bonnet with a metallic crack.

And he stalked over to the industrial sink and washed his hands.

Giving her a chance to breathe. And give herself a good talking-to.

What the heck is wrong with you, kid? You know that flirting with him is counter-productive! Is it the reflections in the oil spills you find overly stimulating? Or the winch chains waving in the breeze?

Next time she tracked him down, she'd do so in daylight. *With* an audience. And she'd certainly make sure she kept physical distance between them as well. Whatever it took to keep the heat blooming between them at bay.

She couldn't let herself fall for him again. Even a little bit. Because when she fell, she had a bad habit of becoming who she thought her partner wanted her to be. Surpressing her needs so that they might love her back. A survival skill learned living by the changeable whims of her dearest mother.

That was how things had gone down with The Chef. Even while he'd turned out to be a liar and a cheat, the break-up wasn't entirely on him. If she'd stood up for herself sooner, if she'd laid claim to her life from the very beginning, things wouldn't have ended as they had. In all likelihood they'd have ended before they'd even begun.

But the harder truth was, she'd probably been that way with Rafe the first time around too. *The only time around,* she reminded herself. They'd been so close, she'd not known quite where Rafe ended and she began.

Feet firmly back on the ground, she watched Rafe move about the space. Switching off machinery. Lights. Checking everything was safe. Secure. So self-assured, capable, resilient, sturdy. No wonder she'd been so smitten.

But now those qualities were no longer reasons to want him, but reasons to want her child to be half him.

When he looked over, and the darkness in his eyes made her blood go from normal to full sizzle in half a second, she took a step back.

"I should go," they both said, at the exact same time.

Sable laughed, the sound a little strained. While Rafe simply looked at her. Into her.

Then he slowly strode her way.

She held her breath, waiting for his next words. Bracing herself. Readying to battle, if she needed to.

When he surprised her by saying, "I'm meant to be in Sydney right now."

"Oh?"

He ran a hand up the back of his head, catching on the hair tie and yanking it loose, his curls falling around his face making him look a complete rogue. "There's a refurbed Pontiac in my Surry Hills shop, owned by a Texan ex-pat who is road-trip-happy. Paid extra to make sure I signed off on the completion, in person. Yet here I am."

Sable had no idea what to say.

Rafe, on the other hand, wasn't done. "Later tonight, I'm meant to be on a flight to Dubai where I was to have first eyes on a Mustang GT Cobra Jet, which one of the royals found under a tarp in his father's other palace."

Lots to digest there, but Sable found herself stuck on the "Was? Meaning no longer. Because you're here. You're here because of me."

He nodded. But he didn't look disapproving. Or disappointed. Or stunned and confused as he had back at the fairground that morning.

He looked as if he could hear the whump-whump-whump of the blood pulsing through her. As if he too could taste the sensual tension in the air, above and beyond the tang of oil and steel. He looked as if it was taking every ounce of restraint to hold himself back too.

Then Rafe muttered, "To hell with it," before

he took three long strides, reached a hand around her waist and hauled her close.

Sable's breath left her in a whoosh. Her thoughts following straight after. Until she was nothing but nerves and heat and a frantic pulse.

Then with a growl that sounded as if it came from the very deepest place inside him, Rafe leaned in and kissed her.

No hesitation. No softness. No finding his way.

He kissed her with a decade's worth of built-up heat. And anger. And frustration. She felt it all. Every feeling, every drop of heartache, every wave of disbelief.

Sable couldn't have prepared herself for such a kiss if she'd had a lifetime to try.

Sliding a hand around his neck, delving into his curls, she found herself swept away on an ocean of sensation as Rafe held her tighter. Kissed her harder. Heat rose within her, like a storm. A volcano. A rush of memory. And want.

This, her heart sang. *This is what you've been missing for so long. This is what you want! Him.*

All her sweetest memories were wrapped up in this man's smiles, and she wanted to have his baby, and it had been eons since she'd been kissed with such…thoroughness. Who said she couldn't have her cake and eat it too?

Her hand gripped the front of his shirt to drag him closer as the kiss deepened. Fuelled by regret and sorrow and punishment and mistakes they both clearly needed to fill with something more joyful.

Rafe's hand moved. She whimpered at the loss. Only to feel it slide back around her waist, beneath her coat, beneath her jumper, to find the edge of her waist. Bare skin.

The rough pads of his fingers—familiar yet changed—created waves of sensation, rocketing through her.

How long since she'd been touched like this? Since she'd felt wanted. For nothing but her skin, her warmth, her kiss.

It was heady. A rush. A wondrous thing. She hadn't even realised how much she missed that part of herself. Raw and honest and needy. Rich veins of need. Needing to be closer, to be a part of him, she lifted her leg to wrap itself around his.

Rafe growled, the sound echoing in her chest. Taking her under, till she could no longer hang onto a single thought—

Sable froze, hand at his chest now pressing flat as she tipped her head down, as she drew in a much-needed breath. It took every ounce of effort she had left to cleave herself away.

Rafe's hand slid out of her hair, his fingers so deeply entangled they caught. His hold disappeared from her waist. The loss of each touch felt a little death.

She waited for him to move back, away, to curse himself for giving in. But his hands lifted to hold her by her upper arms, gently, kindly, and she realised how wobbly she was on her feet.

"You okay?" he asked, a glint in his eye as if he knew exactly what he'd just done to her.

"No! Of course I'm not okay! I don't want this. Not from you."

She felt his fingers lift a smidge.

"Could have fooled me."

Sable squeezed her eyes shut. "I didn't mean it that way. I mean, I *did*. But we can't be kissing, Rafe. Kissing complicates things. And I need this—*us*—to be as clear-cut as can be."

A muscle twitched under his right eye. "Because all you want from me is my sperm," he said, his voice a rough burr.

"Yes," she countered. "Your sperm!"

Okay, Sable, perhaps a little less enthusiasm on the sperm front.

"I don't want to be a distraction, Rafe. I don't

want Janie to feel as if she has to look out for you. Or for people to whisper behind their hands about you because I'm back—"

"What people?" he asked, his fingers tightening once more.

"A few people in town today. You know what they can be like—"

Her words dried up at the concern in his dark gaze. Rafe, standing so close, his strong hands holding her, his dark eyes on hers, his familiar scent curling through her making her knees melt, and making it hard to put her true wants into precise words.

Then she closed her eyes, shook her head. "That's not the point. Don't worry about *me*. I'm totally used to it. Water off a duck's back." *Yeah right.* "The point is, I know we can do this right. If it's direct, honest, simple, clear-cut."

Rafe breathed out long and hard, his eyes shifting between hers. Then he slowly let her go. Took a step back. And said, "Sable—"

Knowing, to the very innermost threads of her marrow, he was about to deny her, she cut him off. Searched frantically through the arsenal of arguments she'd prepared, for something that might stay him. "It's sudden. I get that. I wish I could give you all the time and space you need to sort through all of this. But as well as being an overwhelming ask, it's also time sensitive."

Hands lifting to rub the spots he'd late been holding, Sable took another breath. This next bit never got any easier to say out loud. The last person she'd told was The Chef. And the way he'd taken it... As if it was a blessing.

But this wasn't The Chef. This was Rafe. A good, kind, strong man—which was why she'd come to him.

"I saw a doctor a few months ago because my cycle has been seriously out of whack. I assumed it was stress-related as things hadn't been good for quite some time. When she took my medical history my burst appendix came up."

"Your *appendix* burst?" Rafe moved in, hand out to steady her.

"When I was little," she quickly added, quietly telling her heart to chillax when it began to thumpity-thump at the concern in his dark eyes. "Before we moved here. Anyway, it turns out there's damage. Incidental scarring to one of my fallopian tubes means it no longer does the job. That, plus another underlying condition, it's all a bit of a mess in there. If I don't do this, and soon, my chances only go downhill, rapidly."

She finished with a shrug. Refusing to give in

to the hopelessness that came with the litany of reasons why a child might never be in her future. No matter how well she planned it out.

Right now, hope was all she had.

Rafe remained quiet. Too quiet. It took every ounce of restraint she had not to ask what he was thinking. Especially when she wasn't sure she'd like the answer.

"What kind of condition?" he finally asked, his expression grave.

"It's called primary ovarian insufficiency, which basically means my egg-release mechanisms don't work properly or stopped working earlier than they ought."

A shadow passed over his face. Then he ran a hand over his chin and looked away, before leaning back against the closed bonnet of the muscle car and crossing his arms over his broad chest.

"I thought I was handling this rather brilliantly," he said. "You. Being back. I told myself I was fine."

"Are you *not* fine?"

He watched her and said nothing. Stoic. Controlled. Emotions hidden behind a tough facade. It was a side of Rafe she'd conveniently repressed when putting together her plan. His determination to keep such a tight check on his feelings, when hers spilled out of her pores whether she wanted them to or not.

"Rafe," she said. "Talk to me."

Whether it was the crack in her voice, or the fact she held eye contact and refused to let go, something yielded in his gaze.

"You walk in here as if we're in the middle of a conversation from ten years ago. As if all that has happened in the last decade is moot." He glanced down at his shoes then back at her, as if he needed a break between all the words. "I can *feel* myself wanting to accept it too. Just forget all the bad and welcome you home. It's unnerving. You unnerve me, Sutton. I nearly ran over Fred's foot this afternoon, backing a car out of the garage, because my mind was elsewhere. I lost it at him. Poor kid had no idea what he'd done wrong."

"Ouch." Then, "What were you thinking about?"

The look he shot her was direct. A warning. The sudden memory of his mouth on hers, his tongue sliding over the seam of her lips, strong enough her knees buckled.

"Don't sweat it," she said, flapping a hand to distract him from the thoughts no doubt written all over her face. "Someone today told me they believed *fine* was the most loaded word in the English language. I think it's overrated."

"Really?"

"Mmm-hmm. Who needs *fine* when we could do something truly unique? We can do this and come out the other end better than fine."

His gaze dropped to her mouth again, right as she stopped talking to lick her lips. He pressed away from the side of the car. "Let's take this outside."

"Sounds ominous."

"I think a little air is necessary for this kind of talk. Space."

Right. Good call.

She turned and headed out. Night had fallen fast. She blinked into the darkness when the golden light of the workshop switched off, then the groan of the roller door closing echoed over the night.

Rafe followed her through the doorway till they stood, two lone figures in the great gaping concrete entrance. Pale moonlight poured over his broad shoulders, the waves in his hair. There was so much unspent energy coiled within him he practically glowed.

She didn't think it would serve her cause to tell him that they could be in the middle of a field, a desert, a shopping centre car park and it wouldn't make a difference. Any time she was near him space was irrelevant.

Then, his hands delving into the pockets of his jeans, his shoulders lifted to his ears before he let them drop. "I've listened. I've heard you. Now I need you to hear me. You've come looking for something that just isn't there."

"What do you mean?"

"The kid you once knew, the one you came here to find, I left him behind a long time ago. The scourge that came with being my father's son, the pressure to never set a foot wrong, the burden of keeping Janie alive. That's so far in my past I barely think about it any more. But then the moment I saw you, it all came rushing back."

Rafe's words hit—*snick-snick-snick*—like arrows to the chest.

Sable looked down, knowing she wouldn't be able to school her features. Unlike him, it was a skill she'd never figured out.

It wasn't a no, it was a plea. But could she heed his words and walk away? Should she? In her past, it was what she would have done. Bent to his will to ensure he was happy. But now? She was on a mission here, to no longer bend.

Rafe swore beneath his breath, muttering

something about patience and strength. She felt him near right before he nudged a finger under her chin and forced her to look him in the eye.

"Know what else?" he said, his voice rough. "You're not the same girl either. That girl was so tangled up inside—about her mother, about her future, about what people thought about her. But now…"

"Now?"

"Steel," he said. "Along the way you've found yourself some inner steel. It suits you. A great deal." A quick smile, then it was gone. "But the vision you've built up inside your head, of how this idea of yours could ever work, it's based on a phantom. It's not real."

Sable swallowed when tears suddenly burned at the backs of her eyes. Panic rising in her throat, she dug deep, connecting with those threads of steel that now wound their way through her body, and said, "Let me prove you wrong. Ask me anything and I'll show you I have it covered. I've got this, Rafe. I promise."

"Anything?" he said.

Sable tried to ignore the skitters along her skin at the warning in his voice. "Bring it."

"All righty, then. Where would you live? With your mum? No. That would be a disaster. And not here, you made that clear. So LA? From what I gather, LA might not be a good fit right now. So if not LA, how will you find work? Will you work? Do you still work? If you work, will you get help? A nanny? If not, what if you get sick? What if the baby gets sick? And when you say 'no strings' what does that even mean?"

Once he'd stopped long enough to take more than a single breath, she said, "You done?"

"For now."

"All right, then. I plan to live in New York. Brooklyn, to be precise."

Rafe's frown deepened.

"There's community, neighbourhoods, without the claustrophobia of a small town. Urban suburbia: the perfect place to disappear and simply live. Which sounds pretty much perfect to me. I have a real estate agent on the lookout for an old brownstone in need of some love, near my agent, Nancy, who is also a great friend. There's a brilliant day care on her block and a great independent school. I will work."

As she said it, she knew it to be true. And after months of struggling to feel inspired, struggling to find her voice, it was a blessed relief to have the urge again. No more magazine shoots in Greece, though. She was doing something real.

"But I don't need to work. I've done well for myself over the years but haven't had need to touch much of it."

Her eyes having adjusted to the moonlight, she saw the shadow pass over his eyes just before he said, "Because you lived with him. Your ex."

"Do you have questions about that too?" she asked.

His gaze darkened. "Only one."

Her voice was gentle as she said, "I didn't hear a question."

"Am I your fall-back plan?"

"No!" she said, taking another step his way. Reaching out a hand to him, before curling her fingers back into her palm. "God, no. It's not like that."

One eyebrow slid north. Disbelieving.

But how could she possibly tell Rafe what she'd only come to realise since it all fell apart: that she'd stayed with her ex for so long out of habit? That after the excitement of her first year abroad—the prize, the show, the feting—had died down, she'd been so very lonely. Riccardo had contacted her a month after attending her show—asked her out to lunch. How could she explain that she'd taken that first crumb of attention and held onto it with all her might? Mistaking a roof over her head for a home. Mistaking scraps of attention for love.

When she should have known better.

For here, before her—all dark coiled energy, all strength and drive and goodness—was the man who'd shown her what it meant to truly feel at home. What it meant to be loved. And she'd thrown it away.

But Rafe was onto something. She *was* different now. She had moved on. This was all about her future.

"You were right," she said, choosing her words carefully. "I have changed. More in the past few months than the rest of my life combined. That's what your twenties are for, right? Taking leaps? Making mistakes? Figuring out who you are?"

She must have hit a nerve, as he grunted. It sounded as if it was in agreement.

But then he asked the hardest question of all. "Would you have stayed, would you have had his child, had he not...?"

"Cheated on me with a plethora of women?"

Rafe made no response.

"I'd thought, at one time, that would be the case. A time when I was lonelier than I'd ever imagined I could be. I wondered then if a child might be the answer. Might fix us. But I held back. I thought I wasn't ready, when the truth was I knew it wasn't right."

She lifted her shoulder in a shrug. "Turns out he'd had a vasectomy. Years ago. No intention of letting an accidental pregnancy get in the way of his career. He told me the day I found out about my fertility issues. As if it was a good thing."

"Sable," he said, his voice subterranean.

"Dodged a bullet there, right? Literally!"

Her joke fell flat. For beyond the inviolable, unblinking facade, Rafe's whole countenance was stormy. As if he was imagining all the places around Radiance one could easily hide a dead body.

"You are not my fall-back, Rafe," Sable repeated. Then took a calculated risk, saying, "You're the best man I've ever known. And I've loved this baby of mine, this baby that does not yet exist, in my head for so long, how can I not want the best for her?"

"Her?" he repeated, his voice rough.

Was that a flicker? A softening?

"Could be a him. We'd have to wait and see."

His eyes were so dark now, she couldn't make out the centre. But she had his complete attention.

A husky note threaded through her voice as she said, "Say yes, Rafe. Do this for me."

He laughed, though there was no humour in it. Then he growled, loudly, as he ran two hands over his face. "You're not getting a yes. But—and I can't believe I'm even saying this—it's not a no. What it is, is enough for tonight. I'm going to Sydney tomorrow to finish the Pontiac deal. To get some distance so I can think straight. But for now, let me take you home."

For a moment she thought it was an invitation—and all her girl parts jumped to attention. Till she realised he meant *her* home. Her mother's place.

"Thanks. But I think I'll go it alone." Things had ended well, but precariously. She did not want the chance to ruin it. She turned on her heel, wrapped her coat about her, and walked. Throwing, "Come find me when you get back," over her shoulder.

Rafe caught up to her. "Never know who might be out on a night like this. Werewolves. Abductors. The McGlinty brothers."

"Don't the McGlinty brothers work for you?"

"Right. So they do. And they're actually great boys. If they saw you out and about they'd likely offer to drop you home too."

"Radiance. It's gone all mellow in its old age."

"No place like home," said Rafe, and Sable felt a clutch in her chest.

"You're really going to walk with me unless I let you drive, aren't you?"

"Mmm-hmm."

"Fine. Drop me home. Where's your car?"

Rafe motioned to the astounding line-up of muscle cars under the awning on the other side of the petrol pumps. "Take your pick."

It was Sable's turn to laugh, but hers was real. Like air bubbles popping in her chest. "Seriously? Are they all yours?"

"Till we've done them up and someone buys them."

"Are they safe out here?" She couldn't imagine them lasting a day in LA. Even in the Hills cars like these would be kept under lock and key.

He cocked his head. Said, "It's Radiance."

Which, she figured, was answer enough.

"Lead the way."

She did. In the end choosing a midnight-blue Charger with enough grunt when Rafe gunned the engine she felt it in her throat.

Glancing across the console, Rafe's profile in stark relief, shoulders relaxed, in his happy place, made her ache, just a little, for how things had been.

"Ready?" he asked, giving her a look. A look that made her mouth go dry.

She nodded, and sat back. No longer able to ignore the spark burning brightly between them. Now she simply chose not to act on it.

CHAPTER SIX

BY THE TIME they rounded the bend, and the peak of her mother's gabled witchy roof slunk into sight, Sable was ready to leap from the car.

All that moonlight pouring through the car windows. The warmth of the man beside her. The radio playing softly. It was like stepping back in time. Except she used to sit with one foot tucked up on the seat, the other on the dash, her head tilted to watch him. All cool and capable and hers.

She'd yabber on about some new spot she'd found on one of her forest walks, and he'd listen, an elbow on the window frame, a slight smile on his face. Or he'd glance her way, his gaze filled with enough promise to make her toes curl.

Back in the now, Sable kept both feet firmly on the floor, and her eyes front. But the snippets of their recent conversation swirling in her head did her no favours.

"You've found yourself some inner steel. It suits you. A great deal."

"You're the best man I've ever known."

"The moment I saw you, it all came rushing back."

Then there was the look in his eye when she'd spoken about her ex. The look in his eye when he'd said, "Her?"

The car slowed. Sable unbuckled. The car stopped, and she was out of there.

She leaned into the open door and said, "Thanks! I guess I'll see you when you get back?" But Rafe was already hopping out of the driver's side.

She stood so fast she got a head rush. Or maybe it was the sight of him over the top of the car as he ambled around the bonnet. Swinging his keys around a finger. His chin lifted, breathing in the chill night air.

When his eyes met hers, the edge of his mouth kicked north and she found herself stuck.

He looked loose, as if something she'd said had eased his mind. While she felt all tight and clammy with *You're the best man I've ever known* swimming about between her ears.

Remembering she was still standing with the car door open, she slammed it shut. And made to move towards the house.

"Sable," Rafe said.

She gave him a quick glance but kept on walking. "You can head off. No werewolves here. They'd be too scared of my mother to come close." Then she lost her footing and slipped on some damp leaves. He spun her towards him, an arm sliding behind her back, so that she wouldn't fall.

And suddenly there she was. In his arms again. Her heart beat so loudly in her throat, surely he had to hear it.

"We have to stop meeting like this," she said, trying to break the tension.

Only his hot gaze trailed slowly to her mouth. And he held her, in his big strong arms. It would take nothing at all to fist her hand in the front of his shirt, lift up onto her toes and kiss him.

It could be a goodbye kiss. A have-a-good-trip kiss.

Except he'd slide a hand into the hair at the back of her neck, the strands clinging to his fingers. His other arm slipping around her waist. And he'd kiss her right on back. Soft and sweet and slow, this time. A kiss full of longing and promise.

While she'd melt against him, her lips clinging to his, her body trembling.

Blooming slippery heat and swelling need. Till she could no longer feel the cold. Could no longer sense the night. Till she was drowning in him.

Some last thread of sanity had Sable curling her fingers into fists and looking down, her forehead making contact with his chest. There she breathed for a beat or two. For she would not put herself in a position fated to doom.

Once she could feel her feet again, she disentangled herself from his grip, and ducked through her mother's broken front gate.

Waving over her shoulder, as if fearing even looking at Rafe again she'd jump into his arms, she said, "Thanks for the lift. And hearing me out. And the—" *Don't you dare thank him for the kiss.* "Have a good time in Sydney!"

Then she all but jogged down the driveway and went to heave open the front door. Only to find it wouldn't budge. For where there had been no lock, no handle, now there was both.

"Are you kidding me?" Sable muttered between gritted teeth.

Sable stomped down the steps, and—ignoring the dark shape standing not two metres away—she moved around the side of the house.

The ground beneath her boots squished, and

slurped, sucking at her soles, while throwing up the occasional rock to attempt to twist her ankle. So long as she didn't meet a spider web, a toad, a snake, she'd be okay.

One window, two, three, there. Sable slid her fingers under the thin frame of her bedroom window, the wood twisted and gnarled like arthritic fingers, groaning under her efforts, before lifting a good foot in one heave, then jamming. It had to be enough.

She tore off her huge coat and shoved it through the crack. Then she stuck her head inside, followed by her shoulders, then with a leap she pushed herself through the gap, only to find herself stuck.

For her backside had wedged. She was nearly ten years older than the last time she'd done this after all. And now she teetered like a human seesaw.

Feeling all the feels—frustrated, embarrassed, fragile—she closed her eyes and yelled into the darkness. Then she huffed out a breath and let herself hang, her hair falling over her face like a wavy curtain, her legs dangling out of the window.

"Here," a deep voice murmured from behind

her, close enough for her to squeak. "Let me help."

And then Rafe's hands were on Sable's backside, square and firm, one on each butt cheek as he gave her a shove. She gripped the window frame under her hips and wriggled as she began to shift, incrementally at first, then—like water through a hole in a dam—in a big rush.

Sable slid over the small white desk under the window and landed in a heap on the rough rug on the floor.

"You okay?" the deep voice said, humour lighting the dark.

Sable lifted her head, peeled her hair out of her mouth and found Rafe heaving the window open as if it was nothing.

Then he leaned into the gap, his strong forearms resting on the sill. Long fingers gripping one wrist, the other hand dangling over the edge.

Her breath caught as she took a mental snapshot. Moonlight casting a glow around his shoulders, shadows bleeding into the shallows of the brawny tendons in his forearms, the divots outlining his work-roughened knuckles, the gap between his lips.

Looking part caveman, part Viking, part poet,

he was still the most beautiful thing she'd ever photographed.

"Sable?" Mercy called from somewhere inside the house, snapping Sable out of her reverie. "That you screaming blue murder?"

"Ah, yep! In…my room!" she called, feeling as if she were in some kind of vortex between the present and the past as she flapped a hand at Rafe, urging him to disappear.

But he only grinned at her. Adding crinkles to the edges of his dark eyes, a flash of strong white teeth in the shadows of his gorgeous face.

"I thought I heard voices," her mother said as she sauntered into the room, snapped on the naked bulb overhead, all but blinding Sable in the process. "Rafe?"

Rafe nodded. "Mercy."

Sable rubbed her eyes and squinted up at Rafe, then her mother, then Rafe again. Stunned to find both of them calm and smiling.

"You still here," Mercy said.

"Looks that way," he said.

"Unusual for you to stick around this long. Usually see the back of you before I even get the chance to say hello."

At that Rafe smiled. "Off to Sydney tomorrow."

"Right. Good. How's your sister?" her mother asked.

"She's doing all right," said Rafe with a quick smile. Then, "Thank you. And your tomatoes?"

"Thriving. The marigolds really did keep the grasshoppers away." Then a strained, "Thank you."

Sable leant back against the saggy couch. "I feel like I'm in *The Twilight Zone*."

With an exasperated sigh her mother said, "And why is that?"

"You. And him. Having a conversation. Like normal people."

"As opposed to abnormal people?"

As opposed to you telling me to stay away from the boy next door if I had any hope of making something of my life. That he would be the end of all my hopes and dreams and I'd end up just like you.

"What are you doing on the floor?" her mother asked.

"The front door was locked."

Another ever-patient sigh from her mother before, "Well, you were the one who was so insistent I get a lock. There's never been any pleasing you. Give my regards to your sister, Rafe," she said over her shoulder as she wafted from the room.

"Will do," Rafe called back.

Sable scrubbed both hands over her face, before hauling herself to her feet. She winced at a pain in her hip. Another in the heel of her palm.

"You okay?"

Not even close. "Sure," she said, wincing again as she shifted. "Peachy."

After a moment he nodded. And offered up a smile. With crinkly eyes.

Funny that the brooding dissatisfaction had done it for her as a teen. But as a grown-up, this new-found assuredness of his had her feeling all wired and warm.

Rafe's mouth moved, a slight twitch, and she realised she was staring.

She cleared her throat, glanced away. "How long till you're back?"

"Not long," he assured her.

"Okay. We can talk then, then. About…things."

"Yeah," he said, blinking a moment before drawing away, figuratively and literally, rubbing a hand over the back of his neck as he backed away from the window. "Goodnight, Sutton."

"Goodnight, Rafe."

And then he was gone. The window empty bar darkness and moonlight and a light breeze.

Still feeling a little wobbly after the whole kisses in the garage, drive through the moonlight, Rafe's hands on her backside thing, Sable wasn't sure she could cope with her mother. But she went in search anyway, finding Mercy in the kitchen, cleaning what looked like home-grown kale.

"Hungry?" Mercy said.

Sable grimaced as she pulled up a wonky kitchen stool, the bruise on her hip smarting. "Nope. I'm all good."

"Mmm," said Mercy. Then, "So, you and Rafe."

"There is no me and Rafe. Not in the way you mean." Okay, they were in discussions about him fathering her child but, apart from that, nothing to see here.

Mercy snorted. "You keep telling yourself that."

Sable bristled. "I've struggled to catch you these last days, but now we're both here, why don't we catch up? Fill me in—what's the haps in Radiance these days?"

Mercy just kept washing her kale. It would be the cleanest kale ever at this rate. But that was how she went about things. Loud then silent. Keeping Sable in a state of constant vigilance.

It reminded her so much of The Chef she wished she could go back in time, grab her young self by the scruff of the neck and say, *Wake up to yourself!*

At least now she could not be bothered to play her mother's games any more. "You know what, I'm bushed. I might go to my room for a bit. Unless you want help with dinner?"

She made to push back the chair when Mercy said, "Sit down, kid. You know full well I'm happy to see you. But I also wish you'd stayed away."

Sable laughed. It was either that or cry. Then she sank her head into her hands and rubbed her face hard. When she looked at her mother from between her fingers, Mercy was giving her a look.

"I just never wanted you to end up like me, falling for some small-town boy before you even had the chance to know who you were without him."

"I know that. I do." For Mercy had told her so every single day of her life. Her mother's heart was in the right place, even if her parenting methods were less warm and fuzzy and more steamroller. "So, I went away. And I made mistakes anyway. Some really big ones, in fact. But that's okay, because that's how it goes. That's life."

"Mmm."

"I need you to know, though. To really hear me on this. Rafe was never a mistake. He was kind to me. He looked out for me. He respected me, and wished the best for me. He liked me, just as I was. He was my very best friend."

"And now?"

"Now he's a good man I once knew."

The kale lay limp on the cutting board, as Mercy looked off into the distance.

Sable's heart kicked as it did those rare moments her mother didn't school her features. When she was spent. Or late at night when she had nothing to keep her hands busy. Or when she opened the mail box to find it empty.

Then Mercy collected herself and shot Sable a look. "Don't fool yourself. I'll admit, Rafe isn't one of the worst, but they are good at appearing good, till they get what they want."

When she went back to the kale it tore between her fine fingers.

Sable imagined it would have taken a strong man to dare even approach Mercy Sutton, much less gain her trust. Meaning her mother must have fallen hard for her father. Not that she knew for sure. Mercy had rarely ever mentioned him directly. But it was clear—from her obstinacy, her reclusiveness, the way they'd moved around constantly when Sable was a kid—Mercy had held onto the hurt of losing him ever since.

Till it defined her.

And if that wasn't a life lesson to be gentle with yourself, to forgive and nurture and let yourself grow beyond your follies, Sable didn't know what was.

Feeling a rare moment of connectedness with her mother, Sable pushed back her chair, moved around the kitchen bench and leaned in to kiss Mercy on her cool cheek. Her mother leaned in to accept it. A bare quarter inch, but it was something.

"Dinner's in ten minutes," Mercy grumbled. "Come sit with me even if you're not eating."

"Okay, *Mum*."

Mercy sent Sable a tight smile.

Back in her room Sable saw that the rug had buckled when she'd fallen in through the window. She gave it a yank, only to expose a slat of old wood a different colour from the rest. A slat with a missing nail.

She crouched, and jimmied the thing loose. And below the floorboards she found a small tin box. Inside it a treasure trove of memories, sentimental things her mother would have thrown away in a heartbeat.

A pure white feather. A smooth pink stone. A postcard Sable had once found among the junk mail her mother had dumped on the bench.

It was from Greece, the return address a scrawl she could barely make out. When Sable had brought it to her mother, Mercy had taken one look, her face brightening, then crumpling, before she'd thrown the card in the bin. Sable had fished it out later that night, stuck it back together, spinning tales in her head that it might have been from her father. Kidnapped by pirates and sending secret messages so her mother knew she was not forgotten.

But the card wasn't what she was hoping to find inside the little tin box.

There, having slid down beneath everything else, a thin, gold-plated chain, the clasp of which was held together with a slim arrow half the width of her wrist. The bracelet Rafe had given her for her seventeenth birthday. The same night she'd pushed him up against a hay bale in the loft of his father's barn and told him he loved her and it was time to stop pretending otherwise.

As her thumb ran over the dainty curves of the arrow, she remembered opening the gift. And Rafe's voice came to her as clear as if he were whispering the words in her ear.

"You cast your spell on me the moment you looked at me, lying on the banks of the river, your witch eyes drinking me in. You shot an arrow through my heart. Also, I hope and pray the arrow magically infuses you with some small sense of direction, as yours is a shocker."

He'd been nineteen and magnificent as a cloudless midnight sky. She'd loved him for years, so fiercely she'd feared it might cleave her in half. The thought of spending a day apart, much less years, would have been unimaginable.

But if she'd stayed… What was the likelihood they'd still be together?

If she'd stayed, would Rafe have had the gumption, the time, the drive to buy Stan out? Would he have been as driven to make something of himself, to create the big life he now led? The life that had mellowed him, given him purpose. Or would he have poured every ounce of that energy into loving her?

Her mother had wanted her to leave. To protect her. And to forge her.

But Sable now knew leaving was the best thing she could have done for *him*.

Early the next morning Rafe hooked a left from his driveway, about to head to the airport, when he found himself pulling up outside the house next door.

He noted the broken shingles over the front door. The gutters in need of a clean out. He'd get on to that for Mercy. But that wasn't why he'd stopped.

"Just go," he said.

The car said nothing back.

Swearing beneath his breath, Rafe switched off the engine, and got out. Clueless as to what excuse he'd make for knocking on the door. Asking after her bumps and bruises following her fall through the window? Suggesting she check in on Janie if she was bored?

Or to tell Sable, now, so it was done, that while he'd heard her last night, while her words had made him see how serious she was, his answer had to be no.

And not for the reason he would ever have imagined.

Yes, growing up, "family" had been a dirty word. Just because someone was blood, did not mean there would be love, or any instinct to care, no matter what. It was a choice. One that you had to decide to make every day.

But the reason that had kept swimming through his head as he'd tried to fall asleep the night before? If he said yes, and if by some miracle Sable actually had his child, he could not imagine a world in which that child did not know who he was.

It was the "her".

When Sable had innocently let that slip, it had knocked him sideways. Leaving a crack through which a vision had slipped. The vision of a little girl.

Not dark like Janie, but fair like Sable. With her hazel eyes and his curls. He pictured himself, clear as if it were a real memory, holding her tiny hand as he helped her navigate the stones across the river. The same stones he'd used dozens of times, with her mother.

Picturing that little girl, out there in the world, knowing he'd agreed not to be a part of her life? He'd never agree to that. For he knew what it felt to be that child. To have a parent know him, and still turn their back on him. That wasn't the kind of man he was.

Rafe glanced down the side of the house. Once upon a time he'd have slunk through those shadows, and levered open Sable's window.

This time, he walked up to the front door and knocked.

A few beats later, Mercy answered. Gave him a quick once-over. He gave one right on back, which made her laugh out loud.

She leant in the doorway and said, "She's not here."

Rafe would have bet the farm on the fact she'd chosen those words deliberately. For they were the exact same words Mercy had used on him to let him know Sable had fled to the other side of the world.

"That so?" he said.

"Don't panic, boy," she said, even while he thought he'd hidden the brief flash of it rather well. "She went off into the bush with her old camera an hour ago. Like stepping back in time seeing her with that thing around her neck again."

While Rafe breathed again. "What makes you think I'm not here to see you?"

A smile kicked at the corner of Mercy's mouth. For they'd formed a grudging friendship over the years. The only two people in the world who understood what it meant to have a Sable-sized hole in their lives.

Mercy pushed the door wider and padded inside. And while he wasn't sure he'd had enough uninterrupted sleep to take a Mercy conversation, he followed her inside.

"Water?" she called over her shoulder. "Tea? Tequila?"

It was eight in the morning. "Not for me. But you go right ahead."

Mercy stopped in the kitchen, pulled up a stool, and said, "If you're here to ask for my blessing to start something up with my daughter again you're not getting it."

He could have assured her that was far from the case, but found himself saying, "Don't need your blessing, Mercy. Never did."

"You sure about that? Didn't take much encouragement for her to leave you the first time."

Rafe's fingers went to the bridge of his nose. "I'd be really careful, Mercy. She left to make you happy. Make sure she also knows you're happy she's back."

Mercy's expression twisted before she looked away. "Sooner she gets back out there, the better. She was living the dream, you know."

"Not her dream." For Rafe knew all about Sable's dream. She'd spent the last few days drawing it out for him in painstaking detail.

Then Mercy surprised the heck out of him, her nostrils flaring before her face crumpled, her bottom lip quivering before she looked down at her hands. "I thought she was doing fine."

There's that word again.

Rafe leaned forward, resting his elbows on his knees. "I'm sure she was. For a time. But from what I can gather, she's been lost out there for some time. Did you not pick up on it? When you talked?"

"I wondered," she said, then rallied in true Mercy fashion. "But life is a struggle." Then she crumbled again. It was like an emotional roller coaster. "I never got the feeling that he—that man of hers—was bad to her. I figured he was merely ambivalent."

"And that was okay with you?"

She looked up, her eyes intensely green, with none of her daughter's softness, pinning him with a glare. "*You* were never ambivalent."

Rafe stilled. Not sure if that was an accusation, or a compliment. "Thank you?"

"You want to know why she left you?"

If he'd seen it coming, he might have been able

to steel himself. Janie called it his balaclava look. Instead, his entire body jolted.

"I saw you," said Mercy. "In the jewellery store. You were looking at a diamond ring."

Rafe held his breath as his memories whipped back through time. In the silence, wind set the tree branches outside scratching against the sun-room windows.

He could tell Mercy was waiting for him to play dumb. But doing what was expected had never been his way. "I'd saved for it for months. Years, really. I was going to give it to her on her eighteenth birthday."

Mercy's face worked. "My problem with you, Rafe Thorne, was never personal. My daughter was always too naïve. She needed grit. Resilience. She could never find that inside of her when she had you making things too easy for her."

Sounded pretty personal to him.

"So I told her to go. Told her she'd never forgive herself if she didn't. That I was prime example of what it felt like to live too small a life."

Mercy's background had always been a mystery. But he wasn't going to bite now. This was about Sable. And about him. "Here's the thing neither of you seemed to grasp—I'd never have held her back if I'd known about the prize. Even if it meant letting her go."

Mercy's mouth flickered.

"Not that it matters now," said Rafe.

"Rubbish. Watching you together, last night, the look in her eyes, the look in yours—" She exhaled hard. "If you care for her at all, and I know that you do, let her go. Let her go for good."

Rafe let Sable's mother sling every charge she needed to sling. For he knew that Mercy's hardness grew from a deep, instinctual love for her daughter. The kind he'd never had with his own parents. But even while he could have put her mind a little at ease with assurances, or a blood oath, the promise simply refused to come.

For she wasn't entirely wrong. There was a significant connection between them. Whether it was chemical, or electrical, or some force he'd never understand, it was a connection that distance, time and heartache had not severed.

Deciding to act on it, or not, that was where free will came in. She'd chosen to leave. She'd chosen to return. While he was choosing to... bide his time till he'd cleared his head.

He rapped a knuckle on the edge of her bench and said, "I'm late. Have to go." Then he turned and walked back down the hall.

"I won't tell her you came by!" Mercy called.

Rafe waved in response. Fine with him. He wouldn't know how to explain that conversation to Sable if he'd wanted to.

He'd go to Sydney, pick up the Pontiac, drive it to Melbourne. A good long car ride was the best way he knew how to clear his head.

He might even get onto the mob in Dubai, negotiate an extension. He could check in with his London branch for a few days, leaving Janie to keep on with the prep on the upcoming Pumpkin Festival car show that was happening a few weeks after that.

Give himself some solid time to put his decision into words he could live with.

Sable would just have to wait.

CHAPTER SEVEN

TWO DAYS LATER Rafe rumbled through Radiance in the restored Pontiac Parisienne he'd driven down from Sydney.

The window was down, his arm resting on the windowsill, as he breathed in the crisp autumn air. No other place in the world smelled quite like it. Fresh, clear, with a tangy edge.

Home.

But it wasn't the promise of clean air that had him driving a smidge over the speed limit the entire way back from Sydney. Or the promise of light traffic making him take a left at Albury rather than taking the straight run to Melbourne. It also wasn't the reason he wasn't on his way to Dubai, or London for that matter.

It was the same reason he'd been on edge for the past two days, spending more time under cars than buying or selling, only blowing his calendar out all the more.

He needed to get the Sable issue sorted.

His phone burred. He answered, hands free. "Janie, what's up?"

"Wanda rang, she said she saw you trundling down the avenue, and could I send you her way as soon as possible as her oven light isn't working. Aren't you meant to be in Abi Dhabi?"

"Dubai." He slowed as a sprinkling of swallows swerved from the treetops and into his lane before flittering off into the sky. "I'm sending Jake from the London office in my stead."

Janie's silence was telling.

"You still there?"

"Sorry, just had to pick myself up off the floor. Did you just say that you're...*delegating*?"

Rafe rolled out a shoulder and ducked to look through the low-slung branches of an elm to see if he could find a familiar blonde head in any of the Laurel Avenue shops. "It seems so."

"Am I allowed to hypothesise why?"

"Nope."

"Okay. Look, I wasn't going to say anything, but since your entire world is going topsy-turvy already, you should probably know it's been a little rough here for her the last couple of days."

Rafe didn't need to ask to know who the "her" was. "How so?"

"Some American tourist recognised Sable,

walked up and snapped a photo right in her face while she was eating a pie at Bear's. Big Bear lived up to his name, shooed them out, gave them the fright of their lives, but it was all over the tabloids within the hour. Headlines such as *Shamed Star's Girlfriend Celeb Shutterbug Sable Sutton Seen Stuffing Her Face in Small-Town Hideaway as She Laments Loss of Famous Foodie Lover.*"

Rafe flinched. It was rough stuff. On many levels. Not least of which the jumbled alliteration. "Please tell me you're reading that and didn't memorise it."

"Want to hear the others?"

"That would be a no."

"Okay. There's more. Trudy refused service at the wool store, telling Sable she didn't belong around here."

Rafe tapped the brake hard enough the car nearly stalled.

"I took care of it," said Janie. "Swung by when I was picking up wood from the hardware store to start making the signs for the car show, asked Trudy what the hell she thought she was doing. She blanched like an almond. Said she'd heard Wanda tell Carleen that Sable had done you wrong, and this town looks after its own. I told her Sable *was* our own and to send her some free wool in apology. The good stuff."

"*You* did that?"

"Yup."

This from Janie, who would never leave her cosy little cave if she had the choice. If he wasn't around to nudge her. Make her feel safe. "I'm impressed."

"We Thornes stick together. And now that I'm soon to be an auntie it was my duty."

Rafe tapped the brakes hard that time, the tyres protesting. He glanced in the rear-view mirror to find not a soul behind him the entire way up the avenue. "What's that, now?"

"Ah, right. The auntie thing. Ed let slip when I had him over for dinner."

"Ed?" he parroted. She'd had Ed over for *dinner*? And, "What the hell does Ed know about anything?"

"Turns out he'd forgotten something at work the other night and when he turned up you and Sable were there. Talking. *About what?* said I, being sisterly and nosey. You should have seen his face when he realised he should have kept mum! So to speak. But it was too late. I grilled him. Poor guy folded like a pack of cards. So, you guys are thinking about making a baby, eh? That was fast."

Small towns, Rafe thought, his inner voice a fractious growl.

Sable's words from the other night came swimming back to him. Her dream to be somewhere with the comfort of community but also the private space to figure things out on her own. Somewhere to *"disappear and simply live".*

And in that moment he got it. All of it. Like a snapshot framed on the mantelpiece. He saw her dream as she imagined it, with a clarity that hit like a punch in the gut.

Rafe thanked everything good and holy when he hit the red light in town so that he could slow to a stop. Running a finger over his bottom lip, he tried to find the right words. Then decided the words weren't for Janie. Not yet. "You home this arvo? I'll swing by then. For a chat. About a brother's right to privacy. And staying away from Ed McGlinty."

In that moment, he felt a flash of affinity with Mercy.

Janie huffed out a breath. "Fine. I'll make a cake. Now go throw stones at her window. Or climb her tower. Or whatever it is you old folk do to woo one another."

"I'm not wooing her. And I'm not old."

"Whatever." With that his sister hung up.

The light turned green, the engine caught, rumbled winningly as it picked up pace. Rafe kept the speed down, checking every shopfront till he saw her.

In Wanda's Cakes and Stuff, of all places. Her hands making pictures in the air as she chatted with someone behind the counter.

Something inside him clutched, tightened, and released. Something that had been coiled in a hard knot since he'd driven out of town. Mercy's words, "She's not here," playing in his head like a broken record. As if deep down inside, he hadn't been entirely sure she'd be there when he got back.

He needed to drop the car at Radiance Restorations, fill it up before getting it to Melbourne, but instead he parked outside Bear's, eased himself up and leapt over the door.

"Look at her go."

Rafe turned, found Bear leaning in the doorway of The Coffee Shop. "Hey," he said, moving in to shake hands.

"Don't let that fool you," said Bear. "They've been giving her an awful hard time since you've been gone."

"It's been two days."

"A lot can happen in two days."

Rafe turned, saw it was Wanda herself who Sable was trying to charm. Though Wanda, arms folded, was having none of it. "What is she even doing over there?"

Bear slanted him a look. "You mean trying to charm the hostile locals when she'd much rather be enjoying a quiet coffee in my much nicer establishment? Come on, mate. Think."

Rafe didn't need to think. He knew.

From Janie's report Sable had every excuse for keeping out of the public eye right now, but knowing how hard he'd found being the subject of town talk as a kid, she was out there, smoothing the way. For him.

As if she was a ripple in the fabric of his existence. Rather than a seismic event.

Rafe took off across the street, pausing to let a single car cruise down the avenue, then jogging the rest of the way.

A half-dozen faces looked up from their conversations as he whipped open the door. Sable turned at the last. Her hands mid move. Her mouth half open.

Then she smiled. Her eyes lighting up, as if inside someone had flipped a switch.

As if *he'd* flipped a switch.

Rafe's lungs emptied in a rush. He felt more than a little light-headed. And the urge to go to her, to drag her into his arms and kiss her till that sunshine filled him too was strong enough he had to press his shoes into the floor.

Because that wasn't why she was back. It *would* only complicate things. Just as she said.

Only, now, none of that held quite the same sway as it did a week ago. None of it was enough to negate the power, the charge he felt just being near her. Making his *fine* life look two-dimensional in comparison.

"Rafe Thorne!" That was Wanda, coming at him with open arms. She enveloped him in a hug that smelled like lanolin and icing sugar. "You here to fix my oven light?"

"Not today, Wanda. I've got a sweet Pontiac outside and I promised Sable a ride."

The customers all craned their heads, oohing and aahing at the slick car gleaming across the road. One of them muttered, "I bet he did."

And Sable's smile slipped, her gaze lowering. As if all the work she'd put in the past two days to try to smooth things over, for him, had been for nought.

Done with overthinking things, Rafe did the

one thing that had always served him, had never let him down. He followed his gut.

Holding out a hand, he said, "You ready, Sutton?"

Sable looked at it, then at the customers who were all watching the interplay with bated breath, then back at him.

He gave her a nod. A subtle wink. All but daring her to take it.

Finally, her hand reached out, cool fingers sliding into his as the sleeve of her jacket slipped back, revealing her wrist. And the fine, gold bracelet wrapped around it.

When she saw the angle of his gaze, she went to pull her sleeve back down, but he took his chance to tug her in close, tuck her hand into his elbow.

He ran a thumb over the fine gold chain. Turned her wrist to find the arrow he'd known would be there.

And something inside him locked into place.

Like a lost puzzle piece that had been missing for years.

He opened the door for her, made room for her to walk through before him. Together they crossed the street. Hips bumping. His hand still resting over hers, his thumb tracing the curve of her wrist.

Bear gave them a smile before he slipped back inside his shop.

A few locals walking down the street slowed, gave them a long look before heading on their way.

"Everyone's staring at us," she murmured as they reached the car, taking care to slip her hand out from the crook of his arm.

"Nah," he said, no longer sure what to do with his arm, now she wasn't holding on. "They're staring at you."

Her gaze locked onto his. Beautifully baffled. Rich, mellow hazel. Flecks of grey and gold. The colours of the trees behind her. Of home.

Rafe, buddy, he thought. *If you don't rein this in, you're gonna find yourself in a world of trouble.*

But it was too late. It had always been too late where she was concerned. The connection between them was inescapable.

If they were on opposite sides of the planet, or not. If they had a child together… Or not.

"Rafe?" she whispered, disoriented. "What happened to Sydney? Dubai? Janie mentioned

London. I expected… I don't know… That you'd be gone. A while."

"Mmm," he said, taking the time to drink her in in a way he hadn't let himself do, not properly, since her return. "Thought the same myself."

"So what are you doing here?"

"This." He moved in, slid a hand behind her neck.

When she didn't demur, he pressed her gently against the side of the car.

When she didn't push him away, or call him out for complicating things, he leaned in, slowly, deliberately, his entire body aching in protest until—with the people of Radiance his witnesses—his lips met hers.

She stilled at the contact for half a second, before he felt her give. Moving to meet him. Melting in his arms.

Then her hands delved slowly into his hair, sending shards of heat down his spine. And he knew he wasn't alone in this. In the connection, or the missing. In the disarray, or the realisation it was what it was. Change or not, they were who they were.

Yet the kiss remained slow. Tender. Tinged with yearning.

Their lips brushing. Lingering. Tasting. Sipping. Offering. Relearning the shape of one another. Lost in a kind of hazy bliss, yet teetering on a knife's edge. As if it could tip over into an inferno any second.

A few seconds later the kiss gentled, and they pulled apart.

Sable's eyes took several moments to flutter open. The surprise, the wonder, the heat in her gaze, the way she remained plastered against him, struck something deeply primal inside.

Inevitable.

"What was that for?" she asked, but there was no castigation in her tone. Merely wonder.

"I heard they've been mean to you."

"They?" she asked, her eyes still not quite focussed.

Rafe cocked his head towards the old men on the park bench outside the barber, then the women with their noses against the window of Wanda's Cakes and Stuff.

"The wool-store lady, thing?" She waved it off. "I've been on the receiving end of far worse."

"Janie told me about the photograph."

Her brow furrowed before smoothing out as she began playing with a loose thread in his shirt. "Oh. That. That kind of thing used to happen all the time. I hated it, but had become…accustomed."

He tried to imagine having to inure himself to having strangers come at him, in vulnerable moments, and sell the spoils for entertainment. "How *do* you get used to something like that?"

"It's fine. Well, not *fine*. I used to smile and try to move on. This time I felt like taking her phone and dropping it in my drink." She shot him a smile that he felt, right in the solar plexus. "But it was clarifying. Made me realise I didn't belong in that space, and neither did I want to. Which made me *really* think about what I did want. And…here I am."

"That doesn't make it right, what Trudy and Wanda pulled. This was your home, once upon a time. You are one of us, no matter where in the world you might be."

She blinked up at him, her eyes coming over a little glossy. Before she swallowed and shook her head. "Don't worry about it. They're just looking out for you. Which makes me appreciate how far they've come. In fact, I wouldn't be surprised if a couple of those women have shrines to you in their basements—"

And from one blink to the next her gaze cleared.

"Hang on a second. Is *that* why you kissed me like that, in front of the whole town? Because you were trying to *protect* me? Just like our first kiss all over again?"

Was it? Partly. And partly because he couldn't *not* kiss her. Which was becoming a problem. One he was apparently willing to take on.

"I can look after myself, Rafe," she said, her face mutinous. "I'm not your responsibility."

But he refused to be pushed away. Not without the chance to have his say. He tucked her in closer. She glared up at him. But made no move to disengage. Her finger was still playing with the loose thread near his heart.

This push and pull, this constant humming tension, it had been their hallmark. For their relationship hadn't happened overnight—it had been built over years. Layers and layers of discovery and demand, differences and insecurities, trust and surrender. Some of which had been swept away by her departure, but not all. The foundations had been too well laid.

That foundation had been the one thing that had kept him upright when she left. For all that her leaving had shattered him, the fact that she'd been in his life at all was the reason he'd come as far as he had. She'd seen such good in him, with her ability to see beauty in places others saw only despair.

Would he ever have been able to realise his dream without her?

Without him would she be able to realise hers?

Her finger slid out from the grip of the cotton and laid over his chest. Her fingers curling gently against his shirt. He felt his heart thump, once, twice, a solid, sure, steady decided beat. A response he'd learned to trust when he'd had nothing else to rely on.

And he heard himself say, "Yes."

"*Yes?* Yes, I can look after myself?" Her eyes widened. "Or yes, as in…?"

Rafe glanced over Sable's shoulder to find the over-sixties walking group standing in a clump, gawping at them. The men in the barber shop had now spilled onto the footpath as well. Bear was out there, trying to hustle them all into The Coffee Shop, but they were all far too immersed in the show playing out before them.

"Can we go for that drive?" Rafe asked.

"Don't you have to get the car to Melbourne?"

"I'll get someone else to finish the trip. In a bit."

"Oh."

"Shall we?"

She nodded, her eyes still wild and wide, her head bobbing like a marionette. When he moved her aside just enough to open the passenger door, she spilled bonelessly inside.

While Rafe felt as if the next hour might well determine the course of his life from that moment on. Not only regarding the possibility of a child out there in the world, but the woman who'd stormed back into his life.

With the roof down, the wind was bracing. But Sable barely noticed for her mind was all a spin as Rafe drove out of town, up into the hills, round and around, till she lost her sense of direction.

Rafe, elbow resting on the windowsill, a finger sliding back and forth over the seam of his lips, his other hand relaxed on the wheel, had a faraway look. Serious.

Her heart clutched as a wave of tenderness, of heat, swept over her. Followed by a swift chill as the word *Yes* swam through her head like a fever dream.

For a second there she'd thought he'd meant… But no. Maybe? She'd thought her arguments were very convincing, so why not?

Sable risked another glance. What was he thinking about? His grocery list? Maybe he was still mulling over how he could make sure the people of Radiance treated her right.

For he was a protector at heart. Always had been. Protecting Janie from the mess she'd been born into. Protecting the memory of his mother, a woman she'd never heard him speak ill of, even while the pain of her departure was written over every line in his face. Even protecting his father, mostly from himself.

He'd kissed her, it seemed, to protect her too.

But it hadn't felt that way. It had felt as if a storm that had been brewing for days had finally broken. It had felt like coming home.

And this time, no single part of her leapt up and said, *Stop! We can't! Too complicated!*

Because for a few beautiful moments it had been such pure relief to slip back to a much simpler time. When she was an anonymous girl who loved nothing more than taking photos of things that other people neglected, and falling for the brooding boy next door.

Sable coughed on her thoughts. Then coughed some more.

Rafe shot her a look. "You okay?"

She gave him a thumbs up, even though she wasn't sure that was entirely true.

She'd only been caught up in a memory of feeling, not actually feeling those feelings, right? For surely the worst time to realise you were falling in…*something* with someone, was not the time to have a baby with them. How twisty was that?

Were her crumbling defences inevitable, or was she self-sabotaging? Was this whole thing a prime example of her putting herself in a "situation doomed to fail", as her ex's enabling therapist had so kindly put it?

"I'm just going to put the car away," Rafe said, slowing as the edge of his property appeared. They'd come around the back way, not past her mother's house.

"Sure," Sable squeaked, then cleared her throat, not sure where "away" might be.

They trundled down his driveway, though he didn't stop at the Airstream, instead hooking a left, past a large copse of elms, and liquid ambers in all their autumn glory, which was when she realised where they were heading.

In the direction of the old barn.

A thrill of anticipation—and trepidation—shot down her spine. If she was worried about how her memories were mixing dangerously with the present, the barn would show her exactly where she stood. For, while she might have blocked out their first not-real kiss, she'd not forgotten a single moment they'd spent in the loft atop the crumbling old ruin.

Memories flooded in so thick and fast she could barely keep up. Holding Rafe's hand as they ran inside to get out of a rainstorm. The scent of old hay. The ladder to the loft. Fake candles making the place look so cosy and romantic. The days and nights spent snuggled up together in their secret place, debating over what their future might look like.

Only when they rounded the trees it was to find the barn was no more.

While it took her head a few moments to take in its replacement—a massive two-storey utilitarian building the size of a small aeroplane hangar—Sable's heart got there all too quick. Squeezing so hard she let out a small noise. Like an ache she couldn't contain.

It should have been less of a shock, for the thing had been held together by branches of the trees growing through it, littered with cracks in the walls, panels torn away by weather, the frame rotted over time. She wondered when it had finally collapsed. Or had Rafe torn *it* down too? Had he exorcised her from his life, the way he had his father?

Heart now beating in her ears, she watched in

silence as a massive roller door in the side of the building opened with a loud rumble.

Rafe eased the car inside. And whatever trepidation and concern had been flickering about inside her disappeared as shock overtook it all.

Sensor lights flickered on revealing what amounted to a car collector's paradise.

Rafe pulled into a space beside an old Bentley. Beside that sat a deep red vintage Ferrari. A gleaming Mustang crouched beyond that. And another. Early models, seriously rare. Car after spectacular car. Some covered in tarps. Others gleaming under the bright lights.

Gaze absorbing all there was to see, she noted a workshop. Down the far end a small office and kitchenette and bathroom. The ceiling was a mile above, held there by a criss cross of metal beams, except at the far end where a second floor had been built in. At the top of a set of thin stairs leading to a closed door.

She swallowed. If memory served, that was also where the loft had been. Their loft.

The car door opened with a snick beside her and she looked up to find Rafe, hand out. She took it, tingles and warmth coursing up her arm. She gently disentangled herself before he figured out, by some kind of osmosis, that she was going all gooey on him.

Then she glanced across to the far wall and saw it. In the same pressed tin as the Radiance Restoration sign, a series of big letters across the workshop wall saying, The Barn. And her knees nearly went out from under her.

Recovering, as well as she could, she asked, "What is this place?"

Rafe laughed, all deep and rumbly, a boot scuffing the polished concrete floor. "The shop is where the bulk of the work is done. This is my display case. I bring clients here from time to time. Temperature and humidity controlled. Special air-conditioning units for dust prevention."

"Wow. The contents must be worth more than the land they're sitting on. Please tell me you have excellent insurance."

"An eye-watering amount."

"Are they all yours?"

"Some," he said with a quiet smile. "A few are here early for the Pumpkin Festival car show. I started it a few years back, with Stan's help, now Janie runs it every year. It's become one of the biggest in the country. Others are ready to be shipped off to their owners. That one," he said, pointing to the tomato-red Ferrari that looked just like the one out of *Ferris Bueller's Day Off*, "is heading to a tech billionaire type from Silicon Valley. The two Mustangs are a his-and-hers pair we brought up to scratch after finding the husks in a shed in Dubbo. Prince Alessandro Giordano of Vallemont choppered in to see them when he was here visiting with his new bride, an Aussie girl from just down the way."

"Who *are* you?" she asked.

He laughed, cheeks pinking, just a smidge, as he ran a hand up the back of his neck. "Now I feel like I'm showing off."

"As well you should! It's very impressive, Rafe. You should be proud of what you've achieved here. Even if you did have to pull down our barn to do it."

She shot him a sideways glance right as his face flickered. His jaw worked. But he said nothing. Shutting down right before her eyes.

"So the Pumpkin Festival, hey?"

"Mmm." A beat, then, "So you'll be here then? Still?"

"I guess that depends." Blood suddenly beating in her ears, she looked up, held his gaze, and said, "That depends on you."

She waited for him to give her an inkling, some clue of what he was thinking, fully expecting him to shut down completely. To go all stoic and statue-like, when instead he held out a hand.

"Come on," he said. "I want to show you something."

Blood still surging, she took his hand. Fingers gripped protectively around hers, he drew her around the bulk of the cars till they stopped before a smaller lump under an old tarp.

"What's this?" she asked.

He tilted his chin. "Have a look."

She bent, found the edge of the tarp and lifted one corner. The hint of small white-walled tyres, with daisy badges on the wheel rims, was all she needed to know what was beneath.

She whipped the tarp away with a flourish to find a 1972 VW Beetle. Matt black paint dulled by time. Peace-sign-shaped gearstick in need of a polish. With its amateur finish, lack of polish, the dents not quite beaten out, it stood out among the cars behind her like a field daisy in a bouquet of red roses.

She'd been sixteen, maybe, when they'd hauled the VW frame, muddy and filthy and busted, out of the creek that traversed the gully behind their houses, after Rafe had seen the striking photograph she'd taken of the thing. The juxtaposition of progress and nature, of death and regrowth, gloomy greys and fresh greens, going on to become her schtick.

And, oh, the days, months, *years* she'd spent happily watching over him as he'd rebuilt the thing from scratch. Rebuilding—as she'd only later found out—for her.

Sable laid a hand on the cool metal, and every emotion she'd spent the past several days trying to keep at bay overflowed. A longing for the simplicity, the surety of those days, so strong it made her sway.

She moved to the driver's side. Hooked her fingers under the handle. It opened with a clunk. Breathing in the scent—new and old mixing into a heady cocktail—she slid inside. The leather seat squeaked as she sank into it. Her hands wrapped around the hard steering wheel.

When, a few moments later, Rafe hopped into the passenger side, their gazes caught.

"You *kept* it."

He closed his eyes and leant back against the head rest. His large body barely fitting in the small space. "Seems so."

"Why?"

"Thought about letting her go over the years, but couldn't seem to do it."

"Why?" she asked again, the word rough,

full of questions she should not be asking. As it opened her up to more than complications. It opened her up entirely.

Rafe tilted his head to look at her. And said, "You know why."

Sable's heart leapt. Her belly dropped. And the rest of her no longer knew which way was up. "Rafe," she said, when she had no idea what else there was to say.

Turned out, he did. "Okay, then."

"Okay?"

"Yes," he said. "The answer is yes. To your request. I'll help you. I'll help you have your child."

"Oh, my God! Oh, Rafe!" She all but crawled across the seat to throw herself into his arms, hanging on for all her might.

Slowly, inevitably, his arms went around her too. His big hands sliding around her back, his face buried in her hair. The shape of him was so achingly intimate. The heat, the overwhelming surety that with him everything would be all right. It felt like...well, it felt like pure happiness. And even while she knew better than to trust it could last, she let it infuse her, let herself enjoy it, another warm memory to tuck away and bring out on cold lonely nights.

When she pulled back, tears now streaming down her face, she found herself laughing. "Thank you. More than I can possibly say. Now I had a great doctor in LA, but still have to find some here. Or Sydney or Melbourne. Whatever suits you. A good one. The best. Whatever it costs. And I'm paying every cent. We'll need lawyers too, for the contract—"

Rafe stopped her there, with a staying hand. "I have provisos."

"Oh." She swallowed. The edges of her bubble of pure happiness starting to wobble. "Such as?"

"I never wanted kids. You know that. I was also nineteen when I made that declaration. Janie was a nine-year-old wildling, still under my care, my father was in as dark a place as he'd ever been and I had no clue if my mother was even alive. Back then, family was a four-letter word." He stopped, picked a stray fleck of peeling vinyl from the dash. "Now, things are different. I'm different. I'm settled. I have structure in my life. Success. Businesses, I've discovered over the past few days, that can actually run without my micromanagement."

When he paused, Sable took a moment before speaking. For she felt, right to the very marrow, that she was a breath away from feeling the first true spark of her dream coming true and she didn't want to ruin it.

"What are you saying exactly?"

"If we do this, we do it together."

A sudden vision filled her head of them "doing it together", making her mouth go dry, and her palms turn damp. "Mmm?"

The edge of his mouth flickered. "Not like that," he said, his voice rough and raw.

Then something flashed over his face that made her wonder if he was imagining the same thing she just had after all.

"I won't walk away, Sutton. I would have to be involved."

"Oh," she said, when she meant, *No, no, no, no, no.*

This wasn't part of the plan! The whole point was, she was doing this on her own. She was finally claiming agency over her life.

She should have known he wasn't the kind of man who would simply walk away.

You did know, a little voice piped up in the far reaches of her subconscious. A little voice that sounded far too smug. She could all but hear it clapping happily at this turn of events.

She shook it off. She *couldn't* possibly have been sure of anything after all this time.

Except him. You were always sure of him.

She pushed the voice deep, deep down inside and said, "Involved?"

"I can't imagine having a child in the world knowing I chose to be uninvolved." A pause, then, "I know what it feels like to be that kid, Sutton. And so do you."

Sable blinked so hard she had to stop in order to disentangle her lashes. "Then again it was the parents who stuck with us who made our childhoods harder still."

She let that sit for a beat.

"Kids are clever. They know when a parent is there under protest. But I won't be that parent. I'll be the mum who loves their kid so deeply they never doubt it. Who shows them and tells them, every single day, how wanted they are. How important. How loved. You know I have that in me, Rafe. You know how it feels to be loved by me."

Oh, God... She heard the words before she could stop them. Saw the heat and the hurt ravage his gorgeous face.

"My point is, if a child is seen, heard, guided, understood, and wanted so patently, surely it doesn't matter if they have one parent, or ten?"

Rafe's gaze was hard on hers as he listened.

Really listened. No dismissing her, or deciding instantly that his opinion mattered more. Considering the myriad people she'd had to deal with in her life who did the opposite, it was a hell of a thing. And while bigger things were at stake here, she found another piece of herself falling into his hands.

"What was it you said the other day?" she said. "That romantic vision you had of me heading out into the world and—how did you put it?—*demanding more*. Well, the truth is, until the past few months I'd demanded very little for myself. It was all so foreign, so fast, so lonely—I went along with anything offered. So, this is me demanding more. Demanding I do this on my own."

Her final words were super husky. But what could she do? There was no hiding this was fraught. No hiding this was emotional. That they were both on the verge of something life-changing.

"And this is me, demanding that if we do this, we do it together. You don't get to disappear this time. You don't cut me out."

The word *again* hovered in the tense air between them.

She'd come with a plan, with bullet points, and

preparedness. And oodles of rediscovered hope. Her expectations higher than any sane person had the right to feel. Now she wavered between panic and possibility. Disappointment and utter joy.

Rafe was offering up her dream. With addenda.

The next step, the next *yes*—or no—was up to her.

"So what do you say?" said Rafe, his voice wry. "Initial thoughts are fine."

Sable breathed out a laugh as Rafe tossed her the line she'd already used once on him.

And she said, "Yes. It's a yes. Yes, please. And thank you. And, oh, my God, I can't believe this is actually happening!"

"You're telling me."

Sable laughed again. "I imagined this moment so many times, certain I'd be leaping for joy. But instead I feel like I might never stop shaking. This is a big thing, Rafe."

"About as big as things get. Shaking is smart. Parenthood should be humbling."

"Humbling." He was right. Right and good and strong and generous. She couldn't wait to see how all that translated into a brand-new little person in the world. "Can you imagine? A girl with your eyelashes?"

"A girl with your terrible sense of direction."

"Yikes. A boy with your sense of justice."

"A boy with your terrible sense of direction."

She grinned. He grinned back. And she felt it. Like that arrow on her wrist, right through the chest.

Rafe reached out, found her fingers and entwined them with his. Then used them to draw her in. And she went to him. For it felt right, as right as any part of this plan, that they should seal their bargain on a single sweet kiss.

When she pulled away, he had a look in his eye that had her all but ready to ask why the hell they needed doctors. They *knew* how to make babies the old-fashioned way.

But her reach for independence, for autonomy, her determination to hold true to herself, could not waver.

Yet here they were. Holding hands and gazing into one another's eyes.

She cleared her throat, took back her hand. And remembered she was sitting inside the car he'd spent years building. For her. It was all suddenly a little too much.

She hopped out of the car. Breathed deep. Happy to have a little distance from the man.

Though distance wasn't a luxury that would last long.

Though they had to work out the exact details, saying yes would likely mean visits and catch-ups and holidays and birthdays, having his input, his help. Being connected to Rafe for the rest of her natural life.

It would also probably mean sticking in Radiance for a little while longer, at least. Meaning more time with her mother. Having to face the Wandas and Trudys out there. To accept that the people around here *would* care about her business whether she wanted them to or not.

She should have felt twitchy. Trapped.

Instead she felt her feet grounding. Her skittish heart settling.

She could handle waking to the sound of birdsong for a little longer. The crisp feel of autumn leaves crunching underfoot. The taste of home-made cherry pie and fresh whipped cream made from the milk of a cow living just down the road.

More than that, the juxtaposition of light and colour, foliage and bark, trickling streams and the violent beauty of a forest reclaiming fallen trees had relit the fire of inspiration inside her. Her daily walks with her old camera slung around her neck had reminded her, up close in full colour, why she'd taken up photography in the first place. Before it had become a job.

Back here at the site of the original crossroads, she was now officially taking her road less travelled. The road to motherhood. Not only settled on who her child's father would be, but getting closer and closer to being sure of who her child's mother was too.

CHAPTER EIGHT

"THIS IS SUCH an LA thing to do," Mercy grumbled.

Sable turned towards her mother, who was chopping vegetables with such vehemence she'd made sure to keep her distance.

"It's so not," Sable chided.

"So why are we doing this?"

"Asking friends over to dinner is a regular grown-up thing to do. It's just that you were never a regular grown-up."

The fact that she needed one of those "friends" and her mother to get along as well as possible because they soon might be related was something she didn't plan to own up to just yet. The others she'd invited as mere window dressing.

It was a few days after the Big Yes, as Sable called it in her head, and Rafe was due back any minute. In the end he *had* driven the Pontiac to Melbourne, probably trying to keep things as normal on his end as possible. He'd also promised to see a specialist there that Sable had found. She hoped the invasive nature of what she was asking wouldn't send him running for the hills.

His words came floating back to her, as they had over the past few days.

"If we do this, we do it together. You don't get to disappear this time. You don't cut me out."

Clearly she'd taken on the "running for the hills" mantle in their relationship. Not that they had a *relationship* so much as an agreement. Terms still under construction.

She glanced at her mother. The queen of disappearing, walking away, cutting people out. "You okay over there?"

Mumble, mumble. "Can't cook and she throws a dinner party." *Mumble, mumble.*

"I lived with a world-famous chef for years. Chances are I picked up a thing or two."

Mercy stopped, shot her a sharp look, thoughts tumbling over behind her vivid eyes. "And how was that?"

"Which part, exactly? LA? Living with a chef?"

"Take your pick." Mercy waved a hand her way. The one holding a knife, naturally.

Sable found herself looking for her mother's motivation in asking. The ulterior motive. For she never—ever—asked such open questions.

But this was her future child's grandmother. If there was ever a time to accept an olive branch, this was it.

"New York was great. But LA? The light was different somehow," said Sable, starting slow, "which made everything feel a little unreal. For quite a while, actually. As to living with a chef…" She shrugged, feeling a little squally. She pressed her shoulders back. That part of her past was done.

While Rafe's part in her past, present, future, would never be done.

There it was, that cheeky little voice again. It had been piping up more and more over the past few days.

She glanced at her mum to find Mercy still watching her. Carefully.

"Was he kind to you at all?" her mother asked, gripping the knife handle tighter.

Sable blinked. "Um, yes. Of course. I wouldn't have stuck around so long if he wasn't. He was… nice. He told me he loved me, but I think what he loved was my work. He raved about my photographs. But with me he was…detached. A complete turnabout from how intense everything had been back here. Which, at first, was a relief. But after a while I craved the rawness, the honesty, the directness I was used to."

Sable nudged a hip against the bench.

"And while we may have different ideas on what my life should look like, I've never for a second doubted your love. So thank *you*. For that. I now know just how much better that is than the alternative."

Mercy swallowed. Sable gave her mother a smile.

"Now get out of my kitchen," Mercy said, quickly swiping a finger beneath each eye. "Before you do something truly LA and skip the salt and sugar."

Everyone arrived en masse, right on the dot of seven, as if they'd all heard about dinner parties but this was their first. Stan, moustache trimmed for the occasion. Bear, looking twice as big as usual without his apron. The McGlinty brothers and their mother Carleen bearing bottles of wine. And lastly, Janie.

And Rafe.

Dark jeans, dark jacket, white T-shirt. Dark hair curling about his cheeks. Dark eyes boring into hers. He could have been the poster boy for bad boys who grew up good. And the moment his eyes met hers, Sable felt the floor dip under her.

"Hey, Sable!"

Sable flinched as Janie leapt in between them, giving her a huge squeeze. And a wink.

She knows, Sable thought, her heart suddenly hammering. *How does she know? Did he tell her? Surely not.*

Then Janie was off, heading into the kitchen. To Mercy. And soon the two of them were chatting and laughing like old friends.

Leaving Sable and Rafe. Alone in the entrance. Starlight poured through the gaps in the overhanging trees beyond, darkness and muffled laughter at Sable's back.

"Hi," she said, her hammering heart now at full gallop. Then she said it again, and felt instantly foolish.

Until Rafe's hard-hewn face broke into a charged smile. Then she felt giddy, and fizzy, and seventeen years old, all over again.

Funny that she'd gone nearly ten years without seeing him, now a couple of days apart felt like an eternity. At least she hadn't said *I missed you*, the words that she now held tight behind her lips.

Rafe leaned in, placed a hand on Sable's lower

back and murmured, "Can we find a minute to-night? Alone?"

"Everything okay?" she said, her voice more than a little husky, hoping his visit to the doctor had gone well. What if it hadn't? What if he had issues too?

"Mmm-hmm," he said. "Everything's fine."

She leaned back to catch his eye, and his hand turned with her till it rested on her waist. His thumb traced circles over the bone. His little finger slid up and down her hip.

"Fine," she said, her voice a little croaky as she found herself all caught up in his dark eyes, his beautiful face, the way he looked at her as if he could keep doing so till the end of time. "There's that word again."

He laughed, a deep, sexy chuckle.

And she thought back to her conversation with her mother in the kitchen and wondered how she'd ever managed to convince herself that what she'd had with The Chef was in any way enough. When, on the other side of the world, once upon a time, she'd had this.

"Rafe!" Janie called.

And Sable jumped. Reminded herself that they were not what they were. What they were, what they would be, was to be affirmed. And that was what Rafe no doubt wanted to hash out tonight. In private.

Sable turned to find Janie holding a jar of pickles that looked as if they were a hundred years old, the younger girl all smiles as she took in how close her brother stood by Sable.

"I need your muscles, bro."

"Later, okay?" Rafe said, his breath catching on her hair, and it was all she could do to stay upright. His hand slowly trailing over her stomach, leaving spot fires in its wake before he sauntered away.

Breathing out hard, Sable looked over to find her mother watching. A silhouette at the end of the hall. Her expression fierce. The knife gripped in her hand once more.

This was going to be a long night.

Sable sat diagonally across from Rafe at the dinner table, watching him over her glass of wine, while trying not to look as if she was watching him. Unable to keep her gaze from swinging his way.

Bear, seated beside her, said, "Hey."

Sable flinched, her knee hitting the underside of the table. "Mmm?"

"Did Janie and your mother do all the cooking?"

Sable managed a nod.

"Then none of us are getting out of here alive."

Sable lifted her glass in salute, and he clinked it with his, then turned to talk to Fred on the other side.

Leaving Sable to not look at Rafe. Her leg jiggling so hard under the table she worried it might jiggle right off.

For her mind had been spinning in circles ever since he'd walked in the door. Ever since she'd allowed herself to admit she'd missed him. Ever since she'd let herself acknowledge what she'd had with him, back then, was irreplaceable.

How had she possibly been strong enough to come back to him, put herself out there, open up, exposing her most vulnerable self, if not for the surety that a single moment of Rafe's unbroken attention had always been worth more to her than an entire city of lights?

For she'd never loved anyone—*anyone*—the way she'd loved this man.

Loved. Past tense.

This, this feeling swarming over her right now, it was gratitude. Anticipation. With a healthy dash of lust. Not the other thing.

"Best dinner I've had in as long as I can re-member," Stan professed, his plate squeaky clean while the others were barely touched.

"You eat at mine three times a week," Bear protested.

Stan shrugged, then sent a moony glance towards Mercy. "You're a fine hostess."

Mercy waved a hand his way. "It's inedible. But thank you."

"So, what are they going to call you when the bairn arrives? Nanna? Grandma?"

Leading Sable to spit a mouthful of wine fair across the table.

Carleen gasped, her white top covered in splat-ters of pink. The boys leapt up, fussing over her. Bear turned to Sable, his eyes near bugging out of his head. While Stan sank down into his seat.

How the heck did Stan know? Sable glanced around the table; Janie looked at her lap, while Ed looked chagrined. Did they *all* know? And *how*?

No. Not all. For Mercy glared at her like a thing possessed.

"You're *pregnant*?" Mercy managed. "To him?" A long bony finger pointed towards Rafe, her tone acidic enough to burn through metal.

"No!" said Sable. And Mercy exhaled so hard

she seemed to shrink. "I wouldn't be on my second glass of wine if I was." Or was it her third? "But—"

"*But?* There's a but?"

Sable glanced at Rafe, who, frustratingly, sat back, arms crossed, expression unreadable. Having gone full self-preservation mode.

Well, it was out now. And from her extensive experience with deeply uncomfortable conversations, Sable had learned it was always better to be honest, and just push through it.

"But that is our plan. We've found some excellent doctors who think there's a good chance they can help make it happen, so hopefully, soon, yes, I'll be pregnant with Rafe's baby."

"What the heck do they need doctors for?" That was Ed.

Janie shrugged. "Beats me."

The faces around the table ranged from shock to discomfort. How had they gone from *"Please pass the salt"* to this?

"We're not together," she went on, in it now. "We're not in a relationship. Rafe has kindly agreed to do this for me. It's a…" What was it they were doing exactly? "It's a transaction?"

If Rafe looked rock-like before, at Sable's

transaction comment, he now looked positively petrified.

"They want to have a baby together without the fun part?" Ed muttered, though loudly enough for everyone to hear. "Makes no sense."

Janie's, "I know, right," just as clear.

Before Sable could dig herself deeper into a hole of too much information, Mercy pushed back her chair with such vehemence it wobbled, spun and crashed to the ground. Then she swept from the room, her skirt floating behind her.

"Excuse me," Sable said, motioning to Bear to take over. Which he did, his voice following her down the hall, "Right, people. Anyone know if Mercy stocks soda water?"

Sable found her mother in her bedroom, a hand on the desk beneath the window, fingers splayed over a slew of early photos Sable had taken that she'd found in a box at the top of a cupboard. "Mum?"

Mercy looked up. Her face pinched. Pained. "What the hell are you thinking?"

Sable moved slowly into the room.

"You had it so good," her mother muttered. "Away from here. Away from him."

Sable shook her head. "Maybe I was too subtle before. Things were not good for most of the time I was over there. Most of the time I felt as if I couldn't move, couldn't smile, couldn't breathe."

"Then go somewhere else! Try something else!"

"I am trying something else. I'm trying listening to myself. Listening to my needs, to my voice. I'm trying what I want for once. I want a child, Mum. More than one, if the fates decide. I want a home, with a backyard, and a sprinkler my kids can play under. I want to put down roots. I want my local barista to know how I take my coffee because I go to his coffee shop every morning, not because he saw a picture on Instagram."

The fact that the house that flashed into mind looked very much like the kind you'd find in the small snow towns of Victoria, rather than a Brooklyn brownstone, sent a little shiver through her.

Her mother sniffed. "So this is how you choose to rebel."

Sadie threw her hands in the air. "Oh, damn it, Mum, this is not about you!"

"It's always about the mother."

"Did you get pregnant with me because of *your* mother?"

Her mother slanted her a look that said maybe she had.

"Then tell me so," Sable said. As she knew less about her grandparents than she did about her father, which was saying something. "Throw me a bone here."

Mercy turned, leaned against the desk, her long fingers gripping the top. "*Fine.* My mother was terribly conservative. All baking and aprons and gingham curtains. It was claustrophobic. I couldn't wait to leave home. I had that scholarship to study agriculture at Melbourne Uni. I'd imagined myself a vintner. Then your father came along, all wilful and wild. I saw my way out."

Sable's heart clutched at the tragic note in her mother's voice even while she tried so hard to appear unmoved by her own story. Her story, which did not end well, Mr Wilful and Wild leaving her when he found out she was pregnant.

Sable's voice was raw as she said, "Funny. That I was so desperate to *have* a home, to stay in one place for any length of time, I'd have happily sewn my feet to the floor."

Mercy's right eye flickered. "Sable. Don't do this. Don't place your happiness in the hands of a man."

"I'm not. I'm placing my happiness in my hands. I just need Rafe to help me. And he's agreed. Because he's that good a guy. Just because my father didn't keep his bargains, doesn't mean Rafe would do the same."

Mercy finally looked her way, dismay etched into her features. "You love him, don't you? You love him still."

Sable didn't answer that. She'd only just started wondering the same thing herself. It would mess things up terribly. And if it turned out to be true, that was a conversation to be had between Rafe and her. If she told him at all.

"A baby," Mercy said, her eyes glazed. "How did *they* all know? While I was left in the dark?"

Sable went to her mother and took her by the hand to find the fingers cold, lean, rough. "It wasn't deliberate, I promise. I actually have no idea who knows or how. For this is all very new for us too. And I didn't talk to you about it, because I knew you wouldn't approve."

"Since when have you ever cared about my approval?"

"Since always! You just never wanted me to."

Mercy gave her a look then, as if she'd only just realised how thoroughly she'd hobbled her own efforts.

"Do you know why I left? Why I chose to go to New York?"

"Well, the prize, which you totally deserved. And because I saw Rafe buying the ring and made it crystal clear you would not have my blessing."

Sable shook her head. Then she crouched to the floor, lifted the corner of the rug, and unhooked the floorboard. Pulling out the small metal box, she found the postcard from Greece.

The look on Mercy's face as she took the card in hand was one Sable had never seen before. Shock, heartache, and joy. "Where did you—"

"I took it out of the bin after you threw it away. You were so miserable that week. And I knew the signs. You were about to pack us up and leave again. But I knew how much you loved it here. That you'd put down roots in a way I'd never seen before. So I left instead."

Mercy stared at her daughter.

"I'd seen them over the years, the postcards. No signature. I usually found them torn in half, in the bottom of the bin. It's from him, isn't it? My dad."

"How could you possibly—" Mercy slapped a hand over her mouth. Then her face crumpled.

So shocked was she at seeing her mother in

tears, Sable moved in beside her, wrapped an arm about her mother's bony shoulders.

Finally her mother said, "It's his way of letting me know he's still around. But he was worse at sticking than even me."

Oh, Mercy. "But you loved him anyway."

"A little."

"Still?"

That earned her a smile. "Touché."

When the air in the room settled, Sable drew back. "I'd better go out there, see to our guests."

Her mother waved her away. "Go."

At the door Sable turned. "There is one guest I know would be devastated to think he'd upset you."

Mercy sniffed.

"Stan's pretty hot, don't you think? In a silver fox kind of way."

Mercy shot her a look, and the vulnerability behind it gave Sable hope.

Sable left her mother with the postcard and went back out into the fray.

The McGlintys were gone. Bear too. As he'd been their designated driver.

Janie was saying goodbye to Stan who gripped his hat hard in his hand.

Sable gave him a wave. And a smile. Mouthed, Not your fault.

He nodded, then hobbled out of the front door and was gone.

"Rafe?" Sable asked.

Janie pointed towards the back door, then headed into the kitchen to wash up, singing under her breath. High drama her base normal.

Sable found Rafe in the yard, holding a rope swing that was now a frayed rope, squares of light from the sunroom windows making shapes on the patchy dirt. His fingers gripping tightly, his shoulders a hard line, his profile deadly serious.

Her scalp prickled. Her chest tightened. And everything that had felt so certain an hour before felt wobbly.

He was an intensely private man, who hated nothing more than people sticking their noses in his business.

They hadn't discussed if or how they'd let anyone know, even their families, and in an effort at assuaging her discomfort, she'd just blurted their most private news to some of the biggest gossips in town. She, who knew how it felt to be on the receiving end of whispers and stares.

Badly done, Sable.

And while she'd told her mother Rafe would never back out on a promise, she felt a frisson of very real fear that she'd ruined everything. That it *was* a thing she did! Had her plan to try to bring everyone a little closer, to consolidate the relationships between those who would be a part of her baby's life, instead blown it all apart?

Sable took a step his way and felt time shimmer.

In her mind's eye the blackberries disappeared, the swing was fixed, and Rafe stood barefoot on the lush green grass, shoulders relaxed. She moved in and all but felt herself wrap her arms around his waist, lay a kiss on his shoulder, tuck her head into the warmth of his back. Then came the happy squeal of a child, and a head full of floppy blonde curls came bouncing their way...

Another step and the vision fractured, the grey autumnal evening gloom of this timeline slamming sharply into focus. And she ached, all over, from the loss.

"Rafe?"

He turned, his face unreadable. "Hey."

"Before you say anything, please let me apologise."

"For?" Rafe asked, his voice soft and rough in

the semi-darkness. But closer. It definitely felt as if he'd moved closer.

"My unintended announcement! Stan feels so awful, I ruined Carleen's dress, my mother is sitting in my bedroom being all sentimental—"

"Mercy," he deadpanned. "Sentimental."

She shook her head, her throat too full to speak. "Rafe, stop. Let me say this, please." As if a veil had been lifted she finally let herself see just how much she'd imposed on this man. Not only in the last weeks, but her entire life. "I'm sorry…for everything. My intention was to quietly slip back into your life, and instead I landed like a bomb. Disrupting your business, your reputation in this town. I've forced you to relive a past you've taken great pains to put behind you. And I've asked something of you no sane person would ever ask another—"

"Sable."

"No. It's me. It's my MO. Best of intentions, worst choices. My ex's therapist claimed I deliberately put myself in situations that are doomed to fail. I thought he was a sham, but I'm starting to wonder if he was right."

"Sable."

"Yes?"

Sable looked up to find Rafe had indeed moved

closer. Moonlight poured over his back, creating a halo of silvery light around his big shoulders. His strong arms. How her libido could still yearn for him, even as every other part of her ached for the loss she felt was surely coming, she had no clue.

"Don't much want to talk about your mother right now. Or your fool of an ex. Or his therapist, for that matter. I do want to talk about us."

Sable closed her eyes. To think they'd come so close… "I knew it. You've changed your mind."

"What? No."

"Oh." *Oh!* Her eyes sprang open. "Really?"

"Sable. Once I've made a decision, I stick to it. Simple as that."

"Oh, thank you. Thank you, thank you! I love you so much! I mean, I don't *love* you…" *Oh, heck, how had that slipped out?* "I'm just…" *Mortified!* "Grateful. So deeply grateful…"

Her voice trailed away pathetically at the end, while the tension between them only built as the word she'd dropped swirled around them.

His voice was deeper, lit with a thrum of tension that sang in her blood, when he said, "When I collared you in the hall, I asked if we could find a moment alone."

"Mmm-hmm?"

"I wanted to talk to you about my visit to the doctors in Melbourne—"

"Are you okay?"

"I'm fine. My swimmers are strong and plentiful."

Of course, they were.

"But as I went from listening to the psychologist, to being poked by the fertility specialist, prodded by the ultrasound guy I wondered more and more what I was even doing there."

Sable felt as if she were driving on a never-ending roundabout. Was he about to tell her something good or something bad?

Rafe stepped in, took her by the hand. "Can we agree any attraction between us is not completely in the past?"

Sable blinked at the change of tack. Her gut cried out, *Deny, deny, deny!* But she'd have looked like an idiot. "It's not in the past."

"Great. Now whether it's an echo of what we had, or a glimpse of something new, I'm not sure. But it's there. Constantly. A hum keeping me awake nights."

"Like tinnitus?"

Rafe's face broke into a rare grin and the backs of Sable's knees tingled.

"It's driving me crazy, Sutton. You, being so

near, and me not able to touch you, to hold you, to kiss you. Tell me you feel it too."

Feel it? It was rocketing through her like a sugar rush.

She nodded, feeling as if she'd just taken some huge step into the great unknown space beyond the borders of her plan.

Rafe's chest rose. And fell. "Great. Then I have a proposition for you to consider. I can't believe I'm saying this, but Ed made a good point. Why are we looking at intervention, unless we find, down the track, it's absolutely necessary? When the regular way of making a baby is less invasive, less crazy expensive, less stressful and far more fun than being poked and prodded by strangers."

Why? Because I'm falling for you, Thorne. All over again. And falling into bed with you would have to complicate things beyond anything I can contain.

"Are you hitting on me, Rafe Thorne?" She'd never felt less like making a joke in her life but if she didn't cut through this tension, she'd self-combust.

He shook his head. "See, that's the thing. I'm not. This is a time for rational decisions, not romance. And with this thing simmering between us, untended, unreleased, we are only going to blow." He reached up, tucked a swathe of hair behind her ear. "So what do you say? How about we make a baby, the old-fashioned way?"

His argument sounded so seductive. But could she separate the action from the result? Would being with him let off steam or show her a glimpse of a false life from which she might not recover. "Rafe—"

"No strings, Sutton. Just as you ordered. Only no prescriptions either. No pressure. We let things happen naturally. And if that doesn't work, we seek intervention."

"No strings." She looked from one eye to the other, searching for a glimmer of the feelings that had begun to overwhelm her, pull her under. But all she saw was pragmatism. And lashings of banked heat.

He meant it. He was being grown up about all this. Use the attraction simmering between them to bring about the result she so desperately wanted.

Rafe... No, *Rafe's baby*. A child. Her child.

It was a very sophisticated ask from a country boy. But he'd been around. He'd lived too. Not that she wanted details. Was this how he felt when anyone talked about her life? Her ex? It wasn't fun.

But speaking of fun, she wanted him. So bad. Even standing this close to him she felt feverish with need. "Is this even possible?"

"Only one way to find out?"

Rafe brought her fingers to his mouth and kissed them, one by one, before turning her hand over and resting his lips on her palm. Then his other hand slid under her chin, tilting it just so, so that he might lean down and kiss her.

There was none of the hesitation of their other kisses. Or the penance. Or the relearning.

It was sweet and luscious, full of longing and promise.

It was real.

So real, tears welled in the backs of Sable's eyes, clogging her throat. Too many to spill.

Rafe wasn't pulling back, he was all in.

After being at the lowest point of her life only a couple of months before, here she was, kissing Rafe, her first love, in the moonlight. It felt so terrifyingly close to getting everything she'd ever wanted it shook her to her very core.

She pulled back from the kiss, sucking in a breath. Looked into his eyes. And found herself drowning in the heady mix of emotion she saw within—care, want, need, lust and determination.

"So what do you say?" he asked.

Rafe. Rafe was asking her to be with him. Something he'd *never* done the first time around. She'd been the one to make the first move, seducing him in the barn on her seventeenth birthday. She had no idea how much that had played on the more vulnerable corners of her mind until that minute.

Then some creature deep down inside her slithered giddily to the surface and said, "Why the hell not?"

Rafe laughed, then, with a growl, he picked her up and threw her over his shoulder.

She squealed, then laughed, then struggled to speak for she could barely catch her breath as he loped around the side of the house. "Where are we going?"

"This is not happening in your old bedroom. There's only so far I'll go for the sake of posterity."

"This?" she asked, holding onto his backside for purchase. And because it was just right there. Asking for it.

His hand reached up and smacked her on the backside in recompense.

She glanced at the house as Rafe carried her up the driveway. "Won't Janie be wondering where we are?"

"Don't care."

"I am the host—"

"Do you want to go back in there?"

"God, no."

Rafe slid her down his front till her toes landed on his boots. She luxuriated in the feel of him, hard and spare and big.

He took her gently by the chin. "I've wanted you from the moment I saw you sitting in Bear's café, with a ferocity that has eaten me from the inside out. I tried to ignore it, then to fight it. I'm done. I don't want to wait any more."

"Then don't."

Hand in hand they walked down the footpath, towards Rafe's place. Past the Airstream. Towards the shed. Was this going to be a back seat of a Chevy deal? Or maybe the Ferrari? Did she care?

No strings. Not a one. Just two people with a twisted past littered with battered hopes and two-way heartache agreeing to a no-strings fling in order to make a baby.

As the adrenaline of the past hour began to fade, she waited for sense to kick in. For the bites and stings that had left scars on her heart to pull her up. But this was Rafe's hand she was holding.

She curled her fingers more tightly around his.

They slowed as they reached the big new shed.

"Old barn fell down about a month after you left," Rafe said. "As if it was holding on just for you. Took me a good three years before I was ready to lug the rotting lumber away."

Sable leant her head against his meaty shoulder. So he hadn't torn it down. Hadn't exorcised any memories of her. He'd held on. Perhaps he was still holding on. Perhaps she was too.

Only now she knew she'd never let go. Not if he couldn't go through with it. Not if this experiment failed. He'd always be a part of her. Her Rafe.

Needing to show him how much she was feeling, she drew him in, and kissed him with everything she had.

He slid a hand under her knees. Picked her up and carried her over the threshold. In the back of her mind she saw sensor lights, zillion-dollar cars and stairs, but nothing mattered bar the heat and shivery skin and heavy breaths.

He pushed open the door and carried her into the new loft space.

"Our window," she whispered, spying the large round window filling much of the far wall.

Rafe glanced over his shoulder. "Our window smashed into a thousand pieces when the building went down."

"And yet that one looks very much the same."

Sable's gaze swept back to Rafe, who didn't deny it. He could have put anything on the space the old barn had been, but had chosen to rebuild. Modernising, yet keeping the parts that had been special to him. To them.

He'd loved her once. More than she'd ever thought it was possible to be loved. And she'd left him. Sacrificed what they'd had to give her mother the sense of place Mercy had always craved.

Now it was her turn.

As that last grip on her past self fell away, Sable felt free. Free to want and ask and be and feel.

And if she hadn't already known she was falling for Rafe Thorne, the bad boy next door, all over again—if she'd ever really fallen out—she knew then.

Rafe tossed her onto a big soft bed.

She reached for him as he climbed over her,

teeth nipping at her hip, then tugging at the edge of her top, sending her senses scattering.

When she got the chance, she tore his jumper over his head. Went for the fly of his jeans. He stopped her with a smile, with a waggle of his eyebrows, then a kiss that made her boneless.

Only then did he undress her. Slowly. Deliberately. Reverently. Following every slide of fabric with a trail of kisses. His gaze hungry. His touch tender. Till she could no longer think.

Just enough to do the same to him. Fingers trailing over the strong muscles of his shoulders. A scar on his left pec, another, longer, on his side. Marks of a life lived hard. Tough. A survivor.

When she shivered, he drew the blankets over them both, and slid down her body, kissing her neck, her breasts, each rib as he made his way down.

Sable reached back, one hand gripping a heavy iron railing on the bedhead, the other clutching a hunk of blanket as his tongue dipped into her belly button. Licked the edge of her hipbone. Lower.

The scruff of his unshaven face. The give and take of his clever mouth. It was the Rafe she remembered. Times a billion.

She'd been seventeen when she'd left, their love life new, sweet, fumbling, only just figuring one another out.

This was grown up. Edged with knowledge, determined forgiveness, and a steady heady beat of hope.

Sable's eyes slammed shut, every sense sighing, screaming, holding on for dear life as Rafe took her to the edge and right on over.

Damp and hot and reeling—in primal shock—she forced her eyes open when she felt Rafe come out from under the blankets.

"Hi," he said, a smile lighting his face, lighting his eyes.

"Hello to you too," she managed.

Then she lifted her head and kissed him, wrapping her legs around him, holding him close. Near. Dear.

This was the time to reach for protection. But neither did.

"We're really doing this?" Sable managed.

"Doc gave me a clean bill of health. Call her, if you're concerned."

"Now?"

Rafe lifted his head a fraction to look deep into her eyes. "If that's what you need. Of course."

"I trust you," she said. And meant it. "You'd

never hurt me, Rafe. But that's not what I meant. I mean you and me and a baby?"

Rafe moved his hand to sweep a lock of hair from her cheek. "In the past week I've spent more time than a man should picturing how to adapt this space with a kitchen upstairs, bathroom, a nursery."

"You have?" she asked, all the while thinking that didn't sound like "no strings". It sounded like all the strings. But with Rafe pressing occasional kisses along her neck she couldn't remember why that was a problem.

"Bringing up Janie, I know how unspeakably hard parenting can be. And how breathtaking. First words. First steps. First time she said thank you without being asked." He ran his thumb over her cheekbone. "We're doing this, Sutton."

"You're gonna be a father," she said, her voice breaking at the vision she'd had of him in her mother's backyard. The vision she'd thought she'd never live to see.

"I'm going to be a dad."

Her heart swelled so fast she laughed, though it felt more like a sob. The kind that started right deep down inside.

Then Rafe's expression darkened, his eyes smoking over as he leaned down and kissed her.

It was the sweetest kiss of her entire life.

And was soon subsumed by the heat that engulfed her as they came together.

As if they'd never been apart.

She only realised later, as she drifted off to sleep, that while she'd told Rafe she trusted him, trusted he'd never hurt her, he hadn't said the same to her.

CHAPTER NINE

RAFE STOOD IN the small utilitarian kitchen on the ground level of The Barn.

A few cars still remained downstairs, but the workshop had been moved out, readying to turn it into whatever he decided to turn it into.

He scratched his bare chest with one hand, as he waited for the coffee machine to heat up. And he looked up, towards the loft.

Until a few weeks ago, he'd never even slept there, as Janie liked having him nearby when he was home. Now he wondered if he'd put it in out of some kind of wish fulfilment. *If you build it, she will come.* So to speak.

For there Sable slept now, face down, her hair splayed out over her pillow, and half onto his.

The fact that she took up three quarters of the bed and a long while to fully wake in the morning was new to him. They'd been close for years, and officially together for months before she'd skipped out, but it had been all about stealing time. They'd never spent the night together. Never woken to find the other still there.

And now they had… He'd miss it when she was gone. He'd miss *her*.

For that part of the plan hadn't changed as far as he knew.

Once he'd kissed her, swung her into his arms and all but carried her over the threshold of the barn, they'd made few concrete agreements as to what happened after she fell pregnant. As if neither had wanted to jinx it. Or question the halcyon spell that had descended over them.

The coffee machine beeped. He slid two espresso glasses under the spouts, pressed a few buttons and the scent of freshly brewed coffee filled the air.

How normal this had become. The porthole window cracked open of a night, waking to birdsong. Him making two coffees and taking first shower. Her padding downstairs, late, to pack him a lunch to take to work. For he'd not strayed far since things had shifted between them, working at the original workshop most days. Managing remotely. Watching, with immense gratification, Janie take up the slack.

Rafe winced.

Truth was, he didn't want her to leave. Not that

he could tell her. She was her mother's daughter after all. Skittish, unsettled. But the way things were going it felt…possible. As if they finally had their timing right.

He'd work up to it when the time was right. Tell her that he wanted strings. And always had.

Because he was that fully committed to this project: Project Baby.

As for that small voice in the back of his head that perked up every time they were apart, wondering if when he looked back she'd once again be gone? He did his best to ignore it.

Rafe rolled his shoulders.

She wasn't going anywhere. She was in this, as much as he was. He could *feel* it. In her new-found calmness and in her easy smiles. As he listened in on the video chats she had with her agent, Nancy, who seemed like a cracker of a woman. Watched her talk through the test shots she'd taken on her phone, saving the film images taken on her old camera for when the new series she was working on was complete. In the way she looked at him when she thought he didn't notice. In the way she looked at him when he did.

Rafe heard a creak and cocked his ear.

They were heading to Melbourne today—a final day trip before the Pumpkin Festival was due to take up a whole lot of time. He'd check in with the Melbourne operation, while she visited a photography specialist she'd made friends with, and they'd stop at their favourite Italian Place in Lygon Street for lunch before heading back.

He'd built the Melbourne spot, three times the size of the Radiance shop, from absolutely nothing. In a city in which no one judged him beyond the value in his work.

Sable had been the first person who'd ever looked at him as if he was worthy of a chance. Without her he might never have given voice to his ambitions. Or believed they might actually be achievable.

Not that long ago she'd said, "You know how it feels to be loved by me."

It had been a throwaway line, but it had hit him like a Mack truck. Whipping away any last defences he'd held against her. For he'd known how it felt to be loved by her. It was a feeling he'd chased the rest of his life. The feeling of being seen, understood, heard, trusted.

Then she'd left.

"Come on, man. Enough already," he said, gripping the counter. Closing his eyes and willing his lizard brain to shut the hell up.

For all that he was over the moon that she was

back, the second-guessing was wearing at his edges. The looking over his shoulder.

From what he remembered of the time before his mother had left, his father had been exactly the same. Skittish, jumpy, waiting for it all to go wrong.

And it had.

How much was chicken, how much egg, he had no idea. He only knew it wasn't healthy.

And he'd worked damned hard to make sure he didn't follow in his father's footsteps. Any of them.

Including falling for a woman with itchy feet.

Rafe scrubbed a hand over his face, as if that might shake this internal conversation loose.

What happened, happened in the past. And he'd forgiven her. Otherwise how could he have asked her to stay? How could he possibly have considered starting a family with her if he wasn't sure that she was stronger now? That she had changed?

He grabbed the coffees from the machine, dashed a little milk into his, and padded out of the kitchenette, making a beeline for the stairs to the loft.

The sooner he found her where he'd left her, in his bed, *their* bed, every worry would melt away.

Taking the last stairs two at a time, he hit the loft floor and stopped.

The bed was empty.

The sheets were in disarray. The scent of her was sweet, warm—ripe in the air.

She had to be near. He'd only been gone a few minutes. But the gnawing in his belly—and the knowledge that if she'd left once without warning, without reason, she could do it again—bit so hard he winced.

Then the plumbing hushed as the bathroom sink water ran downstairs.

The air left his lungs in a rush.

One thing he'd learned about making broken cars look brand-new: a lifetime of damage left marks that would always be a part of the car. Niggles. Bruises that would linger deep in the belly of the beast.

And while he would have willed it to be different if it were possible, people were very much the same. Meaning this feeling, this knot in his belly where Sable was concerned, might never ease.

He spun and padded back down the stairs.

Sable knew the feeling all too well. The ache in her back. The slight fuzziness of her brain.

Her trip to the bathroom confirmed.

Her period had started.

She wasn't pregnant.

She'd read up, a lot, on this part of the journey, and she knew how rare it was to fall pregnant on the first go. Or the second, or the third. But the ache—the loss of something that had only existed in her head—was acute. Like nothing she'd ever felt.

Groaning, Sable fell into a crouch and wrapped her arms around her belly.

The vision she'd had of that flaxen-haired child had felt so real. So raw. So right. She'd felt as if it were a fait accompli. As if it were meant to be.

And she and Rafe had certainly tried hard enough. Often enough. Their no strings baby-making fling having blossomed into what had fast felt like something a whole lot more.

Rafe.

She closed her eyes tight and sank to the bathroom floor.

How was she going to tell *him*? Now that he'd committed to Project Baby, as he called it, he'd been reading books on fatherhood. Talking to Mercy about their experiences raising girls. She'd seen him stop a mother with a pram on the street the other day to ask what kind of nappy bag she was using.

The man was an utter doll. No wonder these weeks with him had been some of the best of her life. A glimpse into what things might have been like if they were doing this for real. If they were actually together. Building a life. Starting their family.

It had been a kind of lovely she'd never dared hope might be possible. The way he fell asleep with a book on his chest. The way he bartered for control over the remote. The way he played with her hair as they fell asleep.

Sure he grumbled that she took up too much of the bed. And he was a total morning person whereas she was a night owl. And she smiled at the way he wanted her to check in at least once a day when she went on her walks, just to make sure she hadn't been kidnapped by forest pirates, or tripped over a knotty tree root and bumped her head.

Or run away again.

She closed her eyes tight.

And there it was, that single dark thread running through everything they did. The fact that he didn't quite trust her. It showed in the way he breathed out when she came downstairs. The way his eyes lit up when they found one another after work. As if he could only relax when he knew she was still there.

She'd thought she was the one putting herself out there in asking this of him.

But he was too. In agreeing to her request, he'd risked derision from his friends and family, he'd risked the chance of being the focus of town gossip, and he'd risked letting her into his life again. While he might not know it yet, he'd risked the agony of starting to want this too. And watching it fail.

The thought of putting him through that made her feel physically ill.

Maybe this was a sign, the fact that she wasn't pregnant. A sign to slow things down. Maybe even put it on hold for a bit. Despite the difficulties she faced in falling pregnant at all, that felt secondary to everything else right now.

"Sable?" Rafe's voice, warm and deep and wonderful, came to her from the other side of the door.

She squeezed her eyes shut tight. *Keep it together.* "I'll just be another minute."

"All good. Though we have not a thing to eat. Bear's for breakfast before we head off?"

She had to tell him. The thought of having this conversation in public was mortifying. But the thought of telling him here, in this place that had begun to feel like home, felt worse.

"Can we grab something to go? Picnic breakfast in Wonderland Park?"

"Not exactly picnic weather."

He was right. The wind had picked up overnight, bringing with it a wintry blast all the way from Antarctica. Like an omen. "Let's live on the wild side."

He laughed, the sound smoothing its way down her spine, like a caress. She closed her eyes, but not quickly enough to stave off the tear that slipped through.

Then she heard a light bump and she could picture him leaning his forehead against the door. "Sure. Why not?"

She closed her eyes, letting the tears flow fast and furious down each cheek, before she swiped them hastily away. "I'll have a quick shower and be ready in ten."

She was ready in seven. Tears washed away. Game face on. Tougher than she looked. Tougher than she felt. Well used to making big mistakes by now. Used to having to face them.

She'd never been more scared to face up to one than she was right now.

* * *

As they crunched through the piles of dead leaves on their way to Wonderland Park, an icy wind whipped through Sable's jeans, and Rafe's leather jacket that he'd made her wear when she'd forgotten to grab one for herself.

Turned out they couldn't go into the park itself, as city engineers were running final tests on the rides, readying them to run during the Pumpkin Festival that weekend, so they headed to what they now called "their" playground.

Sable walked over to the swing and sat, the chains creaking ominously under her weight. And she shoved her hands deep into the wool-lined pockets of Rafe's jacket. It smelled like him. All warm and clean and delicious. She drank it in deep, knowing that, depending on how this conversation went, it could be the last time she would have the chance for a long while.

Digging her nails into her palms so that she didn't cry, when she looked up at Rafe he was standing over her, holding a tray of coffees from Bear's. And he looked…uneasy.

"It's freezing out here. And I'd love to get on the road soon so we can be back before dark. Maybe we should just take these home."

Home. The Barn. Too many memories, new

and old, swept over her, making her feel nauseous. "Not hungry."

Rafe's eyes narrowed. Then he placed the coffees on the dip at the bottom of the slide. Rubbed a knuckle over his cheek. Eyes locked onto hers. Waiting. As patient as time itself. Always giving her every second she needed to get to where she needed to be.

Why did he have to be so wonderful?

This was going to hurt like hell.

But keeping on as they had? Falling deeper and deeper? Watching him learn to love her again, while knowing he didn't fully trust her, would only hurt the both of them more.

"I've been thinking," she said, her voice cracking.

"About?"

"You know the new series I've been working on?"

She earned a single nod.

"Well, Nancy's been bugging me about heading back over there, to New York. To talk about the concept with a couple of galleries who are showing interest. And while I'm there I thought I should really start looking at some places in Brooklyn."

"Brooklyn."

"In the street I told you about. Near the great schools."

Rafe crossed his arms over his chest and looked out into the distance. Then he laughed. At first it was a shot of breath through flared nostrils, then it was actual laughter, then he finished with his fingers pressed into his eye sockets.

Sable nibbled on the inside of her lip and waited for him to speak.

"I guess I ought to be grateful you're actually telling me this time."

"Excuse me?"

"Come on, Sutton. We're right back where we started. Is this some kind of test? Do you want me to tell you not to go? Do you want me to beg you to stay?"

His gaze flickered to her belly, where he thought she might be building a baby inside her right now. His baby. And the hope in his eyes was palpable.

She didn't move. Not a single muscle. She was hurting so badly at the thought of having to tell him there was no baby, she couldn't see straight.

If only she'd kept to her original plan. For it had been cool, calculated, devoid of attachment. It had put *her* needs front and centre. And now she was practically living with Rafe. Sharing her needs with his. Getting used to falling asleep in his arms. Falling for him all over again.

Falling? She'd fallen. Slowly at first, trying so very hard not to, and then all at once.

How could she not?

He was Rafe. Her Rafe. Once and always the absolute love of her life.

So if she cared for him that much, why was she putting him through this at all? How could she trap him into being connected to her in the most real way for the rest of their lives?

He'd not wanted this. He'd *never* wanted this! Yet he was doing it for her.

She was more upset about telling Rafe she wasn't pregnant than she was about not being pregnant at all. Because deep down she knew, he'd always known, that she was the absolute love of *his* life too.

But if they were meant to be together, it shouldn't be because of a baby. It should be because they wanted it. Despite any obstacles, or promises, or family influence.

This? Being together but not together. Pretending they were so sophisticated, mere friends with benefits. It was cruel and unusual treatment of someone she cared for more than anyone else in the world.

If he had changed, if he truly wanted this, he should have the chance to do it for real. To fall in love with someone he trusted implicitly, someone who had never broken his heart. To have kids when he was ready. The story of how his kids came into being one that would make them feel safe and wanted and loved.

If she truly loved him, she had to set him free. For good.

While Sable's mind spun, Rafe swore, then pushed away from the slide. He came to her, grabbing the chains of the swing. "What do you want me to say, Sable? Do you want me to tell you I was so devastated when you left the last time that I broke three fingers when I punched that big old tree in your mother's front yard? How I didn't get out of bed for a week. That it took for Janie to finally get me up by asking for food when she hadn't eaten for a day."

Sable tried to swallow but her throat had closed up.

Rafe looked deep into her eyes. And said, "Stay. These past weeks… I didn't expect, when I asked you to be with me, that it would be like this. I'd thought we'd be scratching an itch. That all that tension would dissipate over time and we could both move on. Instead it's shown me what my life can be like, if I let it. That I haven't been fully alive since the day you left."

Sable's soul sang, while her heart wept. If he'd said such words a decade ago, if he'd looked her in the eye and let his feelings pour out of him the way he was now, everything might have been different.

Only now it made her more determined to take care of him. To put his needs before hers. Not because it was easier. Or because she'd been brought up to make people like her. But because she loved him.

"I want you to stay," Rafe said, his voice a deep rumble.

And he meant it. She was sure of it. Making this all the harder still.

Sable sat taller, held eye contact and said, "What if I told you there was no baby?"

Rafe flinched. "What do you mean, no baby?"

"What if I wasn't pregnant?"

A shadow passed over his eyes. His gaze dropped to her belly. His brown furrowing as if he was trying to ascertain her truth.

Sable waited for his gaze to lift to hers. "Back at the beginning of all this, I said I trusted you but you didn't say it back. Do you trust me now?"

His pause was telling. "Trust you in what way?"

"Every way."

He ran a hand over his face. "Have I ever woken up, found the bed empty, and for a second wondered if you've gone? Sure."

Sable felt heat rise in her cheeks. "More than once?"

Rafe sank into a crouch. His hands went to her shoulders, sliding down her arms to hold her by the elbows. His gaze locked onto hers and refused to let go. "You're starting to really scare me now, Sutton. What's going on in that head of yours?" he said, his voice rough. "Talk to me."

She swallowed. "I'm not pregnant, Rafe. There is no baby. I got my period. Just this morning."

His eyes squeezed shut. Holding back emotion with such vehemence a vein bulged in his neck. "So why didn't you just say that?"

Rafe's eyes caught hers, searching, begging her to speak. To open up. But she was at the bottom of a well. His face at the top the only light she could see.

He swiped a hand over his face, stood, and turned away.

"What if—?" she started, then stopped.

He turned back to her, his face ravaged. "What if what?"

"What if a baby hadn't been on the cards?

Would you have let me in? Would you have taken me back?"

A muscle flickered at the edge of his eye. "Maybe. No. I don't know. But haven't these past weeks made it clear? You and me…we never needed a baby to bring us together. To be happy."

Sable swallowed. Believing him. And hating it.

She blinked away the grit at the backs of her eyes. Her voice small as she said, "But a baby is what I want, Rafe. Not a relationship. And while I know we both came at this thing from the right place, I think, deep down, we both know what this really was."

"And what is that?"

"Closure."

Rafe reared back as if slapped. "So that's it? One miss and you're giving up on us?"

"Rafe, there is no us." How she kept her voice gentle, she had no idea. For she could barely believe the words even as she said them.

"Harsh, Sutton. That's too damned harsh." Rafe looked as if he wanted to drag the thunder from the clouds hanging low and ominous overhead and throw it down upon the earth. "You know what? In all the years I've known you, that's the first time I've ever looked in your eyes and seen your mother looking back at me."

Sable pushed the swing back and twisted out from under the chains. Away from Rafe. Away from his glinting eyes. She felt so fragile, so pained. It was nearly too much. So she went into "Rafe mode". Full statue. Giving nothing away. Something *he'd* learned at the feet of his father. Not that she'd tell him so. She had hurt him enough.

"There's nothing I can say to change your mind," Rafe said.

There was. But she was not about to ask him to tell her he loved her, that he'd always love her, that they were meant to muddle their way through whatever life threw at them, together. She'd asked too much of him already.

She shook her head and took a few steps away before his voice stopped her in her tracks.

"Where are you going?" he asked.

"To pack. Book my flight. Nancy will meet me when I get to New York."

"Call me," he said, his voice like sandpaper. "When you get there. Let me know you arrived safe."

And this time Rafe was the one to walk away. In the opposite direction. Into the park.

His shoulders were hunched, his strides long. The mist in the air had turned to drizzle until it filled the air with grey, turning Rafe into a smudge in the distance.

Leaving Sable a clear path to head back towards town. Feeling empty. Lost.

But in cutting Rafe loose, in giving him a chance to find all that he truly wanted in time, she was certain she'd done the absolute right thing.

Maybe even for the first time in her life.

CHAPTER TEN

RAFE HAD NO clue how long he'd sat on the stool at the end of The Coffee Shop counter.

But when he looked up, it was dark outside. The rain had eased. The lights inside were turned down low. The front door sign was turned to closed. And his face felt hot from having been smooshed into his palms for ever.

"Another?"

Rafe turned his head on a heavy neck to find Bear at the end of the counter, hand-drying latte glasses. "Hmm?"

"You want another?"

Rafe looked down at the empty mug in front of him. Remembering, a sluggish beat later, it had contained gin and tonic. Perhaps more than one. Not his drink of choice. But it had done the trick. "Are you even licensed?"

"Are you a cop? I'm closed. I'm not selling it to you. Want some or not?"

Rafe pushed the mug out, asking for more.

Bear wandered over and filled it halfway. Then filled a mug of his own, and held it out for a clink.

Rafe blinked at him. "Don't much feel like celebrating."

"Really? I'd never have guessed. You've been such chipper company this evening."

"I'm never chipper."

"I'd have agreed a couple of months back, but ever since a certain someone came back to town, I'd go so far as to say you've been downright giddy!"

Rafe shot Bear a look. It took his brain a few seconds to catch up to his eyes.

He was sloshed. Well and truly. Not something he'd let happen in a very long time, considering his father's predisposition for drowning his sorrows. But right then, numb was better than the alterative.

Stunned. Sideswiped. Laid to waste. And so damned angry at himself for letting it happen all over again. By the same woman. And he'd been ready. He'd been *waiting* for it to happen. Not that telling himself *I told you so* made him feel any better.

"She's gone," he said, barely recognising his own voice.

"That so?"

A pause, then, "I've told you already?"

"Once or twice."

"What else did I tell you?"

"Not much." Though Bear's eyes flickered away, meaning there had been plenty more.

Rafe figured he was unlikely to remember the conversation the next day as it was, so said, "You know we were…trying to fall pregnant."

Bear smiled, a sad smile. "Whole town knows, mate. It's the way these things go."

"Well…it didn't take."

"Ah, man. That's rotten luck."

It was worse than rotten luck. It was soul-crushing.

When he'd told her he thought they could be happy if it was just the two of them, he'd been telling the truth. She was it for him. She was the one. Consuming and confounding and crazy-making as she was.

But once he'd crossed that bridge, he was in. All in. He'd *wanted* to have a baby with Sable. Not to donate sperm. He'd wanted to be with her as her belly grew. To fall out of bed exhausted at three in the morning to get her whatever weird food she craved.

To hold her hand, her gaze, her heart, as she gave birth.

To look into that baby's face—he'd pictured his dark hair and Sable's witch eyes—and feel the kind of love he could barely imagine. The love of a father and child. The love he knew he had within him, despite the lack of an example to look to.

He'd dreamed of them all together, snuggled up in a big soft bed. Sable more beautiful than ever, despite the dark smudges under her eyes from lack of sleep. He'd imagined baby gates and pet guinea pigs and presents piled under a real pine tree at Christmas time. While Sable took photo after photo after photo.

A life laid out before him like an old home movie. A life he'd craved so ravenously as a kid he'd have given a limb to even glimpse it.

"Sable saw it as more than bad luck. She saw it as an out. Wasn't as keen to go the distance as she'd first intimated. So that's the end of it."

"But you don't see it as bad luck."

Rafe's instinct was to go still, self-protect. But the gin had loosened up his usually rock-solid inhibitions. "I do not. I see it as…an experience shared. The kind that binds. That deepens."

"You love her," said Bear.

Rafe did not deny it.

Bear put his mug down, leaned on the counter, and looked out into the middle distance. "Life can be wholly unfair at times."

"Preach," said Rafe, reaching for his mug, only for the scent to make his stomach turn. He pushed the thing away.

Bear gently replaced it with a very strong, very black, very sweet coffee. "So what now?"

Rafe breathed. And hardened. Adding yet another mental layer to the hard shell around his person. "Learnt from a very young age that life goes on. I wake up tomorrow, slide under the chassis of a beautiful old car and I do what I do."

As he said the words he waited for the usual relief that came with work, and routine, and accomplishment to come with it. The counterbalance to the erratic instability of his childhood.

He waited to feel that sense of closure Sable had insisted they'd both been looking for.

But it didn't come.

Sable. Miss Erratic. He'd never been sure if she'd turn left or right. If she'd say yes or no. If she'd stay or go. She should have been the last person to make him feel at home. But with all that came a huge heart. Emotions so close to the surface there was never any mistaking how she felt. An abundance of vulnerability that slayed him.

It must have hurt her like crazy, finding out she wasn't pregnant.

Rafe had been too caught up in his own hurt to imagine how devastated she must have been. To wonder how much that had affected her decision to push him away.

Rafe ran a slow hand over his face, the callouses on his palm catching on the bristles on his chin as the heavy truth filtered through the fog filling his head.

The first time Sable had left had been on her. Her youth, her inexperience, her desperate desire to make her mother happy. She knew it. She owned up to it. Said this is me, this is how I roll, take it or leave it.

But this time? That was on him.

Do you trust me? she'd asked.

And he'd all but said, *No.*

He'd fallen into the trap of believing that the constant ache in his chest meant he didn't trust her. When the truth was he had been in panic mode. In free fall. Falling in love with the woman in his bed.

Not the love of a messed-up teenaged boy, but of a man who knew the import and the rarity of such a connection, with the innate stubbornness to mess it up.

Rafe had always looked to his father as the anti-example of how to live a life. Doing everything not to be like him. But he'd neglected to realise the impact his mother's leaving had had on his make-up.

Stubbornly holding back on starting up with Sable for years before she'd finally demanded he give in. Then refusing to even entertain her desperate desire to have a family. Had he always looked at her expecting rejection? Expecting her to disappoint? Had he always held back a piece of himself? Punishing her for his mother's mistakes? So that he might never be cut that deeply again?

Sable was insanely sensitive to vulnerabilities. It was what made her art so touching. Meaning she had to have sensed the wall he'd kept between them.

No wonder she'd left. No wonder she'd left again.

It must have hurt like hell to put herself out there, to lean on him, to trust him, to open herself up to him, and to have known that he wasn't doing the same.

The bell above the door tinkled, then, "Is he ready to go?" Janie's voice.

Rafe's shoulders dropped. "You called my sister on me?"

"Thought she could roll you on home."

"Hey, brother," Janie said, scraping the stool noisily beside him. "You okay?"

About to say he was *fine*, instead he went with, "Nope. I'm not in any way fine."

"Well, it shows. You look like hell. What happened?"

"Sable happened." That was Bear.

Rafe raised his hands in question. "Really, man?"

Janie tugged on Rafe's sleeve till he turned to her. Her face was distraught. And...and disappointed. As if she knew it was his fault.

Rafe shook his head. "Don't hate her."

"Hate her? How could we hate someone who loves the someone we love so very, very much? We love her to bits."

"Good," said Rafe. "She's my one and only."

Janie made a little mewling sound beside him. Rafe, big brother to the end, lifted a dead arm and hauled his sister in tight.

While Bear's voice turned gruff as he said, "Hell, yeah, she is."

"She has to know that, right?" Rafe asked the big guy. "I mean, if you guys know it, she does too?"

Bear shrugged. "Did you tell her so?"

Rafe opened his mouth to tell of a time he'd told Sable she was everything he'd ever wanted, but couldn't think of one.

He'd *shown* her, in every way he knew how. Feeding her, holding her, protecting her, standing up for her, spending every available second with her, opening his home to her, letting her have control over the remote…sometimes.

She'd known how it felt to be loved by him.

But had he said the words? *Ever?*

No. Because he'd grown up knowing the sway of words. Powerful words. How they could not be taken back.

"Could it be possible she doesn't know?"

Janie made another pathetic sound beside him. Rafe shot her a frown. *Not helping.*

While Bear said, "If not, only one way to make sure."

Rafe pushed the stool back, only to discover he was not so good on his feet. The world swayed. The ground with it.

"Can you…?" Janie asked.

And there was Bear, an arm around his waist

helping him out to Janie's tiny little modern car with its aluminium frame and sorry excuse for an engine.

"When are you going to let me build you a real car?"

"Get in so I can drive you home, you stupid lump," Janie said with a growl. "And you'll see how real my perfectly lovely car is."

The rest was a blur bar Janie and Bear rolling him into the sofa bed in Janie's Airstream. Someone taking off his shoes. Opening one eye to find Janie, laughing and pushing Bear out of the door, telling him she could take it from there.

Then Bear's deep voice at the door. "Will he be okay?"

"He survived losing her once, he can do it again."

At which point his brain gave up and unconsciousness kindly took him under.

Sable hadn't gone back to Rafe's to pack. She'd snuck into Mercy's house instead, needing to be near her mother. Even if her mother was as mothering as an ice cube. After crying till it gave her hiccups, she'd fallen asleep for most of the day, and had woken to find a blanket draped over her and a cup of cold tea on the desk in her room.

The next day she couldn't have bought a ticket out of town if she'd tried, for it was the opening day of the Pumpkin Festival and every bus, car, bike and horse and cart within fifty kilometres was heading in, not out.

All slept out, Sable trudged into town when the sun had only just risen, her hands tucked deep into the pockets of her jacket—Rafe's leather jacket, to be precise, as all her clothes were still in his loft.

There was enough light to see the entire town had been decorated in orange and purple streamers, orange and purple flowers. Even the street lights in the centre of Laurel Avenue flashed a permanent, thematic amber.

Every shop window boasted signs talking up pumpkin soup, pumpkin pie, pumpkin spice coffee, market stalls, live music, and re-enactments harking back to early days of the town when the gold rush and bushrangers were the talk of the day.

If she weren't feeling so rotten, it might have seemed delightful. A marked improvement on the town parade and pumpkin-judging contest that were highlights of the festival a decade before. Right now, all that orange just gave her a headache.

Sable dragged her feet into Bear's, the bell ringing cheerfully overhead. She breathed out in relief to find the place empty and sat at the counter.

"I wondered when you might show your face," said Bear, eyes roving over her bed hair, her old jeans, her oversized Cure T-shirt—also Rafe's. She'd decided she wasn't giving that one back. A spoil of war.

Slowly, slowly, Sable's head sank until it hit the counter with a thud. Even the scent of a freshly brewed strong hot coffee placed next to her barely registered.

"Like that, is it?" Bear asked.

Sable sat up and ran both hands over her face, tugging the skin over the bones before letting it spring back into place. "Very much so. What did you mean by, 'I wondered when you might show your face'?"

"Mmm?"

"Bear," Sable growled. PMS and heartbreak having sapped her of her civility.

"Rafe was in here yesterday. And last night. In fact, Janie and I might have rolled him home only a few hours ago."

"Bear! Did you get him *drunk*?"

"No! Maybe. How was I to know he was such a lightweight?"

"His father only drank so he never drinks."

"Oh. Oops."

"How was he?" *Angry? Sad? Chatty? Inconsolable? Fine...* "What did he say?"

Bear shot her a wry glance, before picking up a perfectly dry glass and drying it some more.

Fair enough. But why couldn't he be the town gossip? Sure, she was glad he wasn't before, but now it would be so helpful.

Sable reached out and grabbed her coffee, wrapping her hands around the hot glass. She drank deep, letting the smooth dark roast fill the parts of her tears had sent dry.

Then someone broke into her peace and quiet, slipping into the seat to her left. Another someone sat in the seat to her right.

"Coffee," said Mercy.

"How 'bout adding a nip of that Pumpkin Spice liqueur I know you have stocked back there?" That was Carleen. The two had become firm friends after the dire dinner party, connecting over disappointment in their respective children.

Bear baulked. "Sun's barely up."

"Meaning it's practically still night time," said Mercy.

Carleen laughed. "As your Queen of the Pumpkin Parade, I decree it's time to get the party started."

"Yes, ma'am."

While Bear moved to the back room, Mercy threw an envelope on the counter in front of Sable. "This came for you."

Sable opened it up to find the name of a Melbourne-based specialist photo developer on a package. The photos from the original film in her box Brownie. She'd sent it to a specialty developer in Melbourne when she'd hit the end of the roll a couple of weeks back, and had been planning on taking her second and third rolls in person the day before. Before their plans had changed.

Sable tore open the envelope, saw the large negatives spilling out. The feel of them—crisp and cool—gave her a sweet little thrill.

The pictures had been loaded back to front. Starting with the ones she'd taken over her first few days in town. The contrast was heavier than she'd have liked, something she'd work on with the next film, but the composition was fair.

Her critique came to a full stop as she saw the photo before the first she had taken.

"Mum?"

"Hmmm." Mercy took one look before screwing up her face.

The photo was of her mother's sunroom—a ray of buttery summer light pouring through her drying lavender hanging from the ceiling.

The next—Wanda and Carleen and Old Man Phillips sitting around a poker table, laughing till you could see their back teeth.

"You took these," Sable said, knowing it to be true.

Mercy waved a hand her way. Called, "What's taking you so long, Bear?"

The next photo was a stray kitten, sitting on Mercy's front stoop, looking right into the lens. The next, Mercy's view looking down at her skirt with her shoes poking out, the wild colours of the clothing contrasting with the raw rough streaks in the wooden floor.

Smiling, Sable shifted to the next photo, then lifted a hand to her mouth.

For there was a photo of Rafe, putting up the tomato trellis on the side of Mercy's house. He'd built that? Neither had said. His hair was shorter, the dark curls cut closer to his head. The roping muscles of arms were brought into sharp relief by the black of his T-shirt, the hard mid-day light.

Mercy must have called his name, as he'd turned towards the camera, a small smile on his face.

It amazed her still that over the years they had found a way to put aside their differences. But over the past weeks she'd come to understand why—they'd missed her. And in one another had found a way to keep her close.

Carleen asked if she could have a look, so Sable went through them all again. Happy with the stunning contrast of brilliant autumn leaves against a harsh grey sky. The old red McGlinty truck, the back filled with pumpkins. Loving the photo of the shops of Laurel Avenue as evening hit, right after a rain shower, light spilling onto the street creating puddles of gold on the foot-path. The view thorough The Barn's new port-hole window.

Markers of her time in Radiance. Memories she'd take with her as she left.

While she felt as if she'd been hollowed out with a spoon, the pictures reminded her that her time there had been pretty wonderful.

As she scrolled through the last shots, and hit

the last picture, she had begun to see a theme. Different from the one she'd described to Nancy. There was none of the discord that had given her career such a great start. No focus on things lost and broken and cast aside. Quite the opposite.

Every single one of her new photographs exuded warmth, nostalgia, harmony, comfort.

She ran a thumb over the corner of the picture of Rafe leaning against the railing of the carousel. The dappled light. The warm foliage. And could all but see the exhibition title written on the marquee outside her favourite little New York gallery: *Home.*

Sable reached out blindly for her coffee and took a sip. Only to find it no longer tasted quite like coffee. "What am I drinking?"

"Clove," said Mercy, sipping her own coffee as if it were manna from heaven, "spice, cinnamon, nutmeg, pepper, ginger and pumpkin."

Sable grabbed the bottle of home-brewed Pumpkin Spice liqueur and read the label. "And vodka."

"Which is made from potatoes. Wholesome as can be. Unless… You're not pregnant, are you?"

Sable coughed on her next sip. "No. Not pregnant."

Though she'd thought she'd kept her voice normal, her mother paused. Looked at her like a hawk. Even Bear seemed to stop breathing.

Sable looked his way. Saw the sorrow in his face.

Rafe... Rafe must have been *really* toasted if he'd told Bear that much. And for Rafe to even go near a drink, well, he must have felt truly wounded.

"Not pregnant," she repeated. Then, "Not living with a guy. Not in a relationship. Just not."

What a mess.

"Drink up," Carleen insisted.

And Sable did as she was told, figuring she had nothing else to lose.

An hour and two espresso cups later Sable was nursing a bruised heart *and* a sore head. The constant low roar of vintage engines, as entrants in the classic car show rumbled down the street, didn't help the latter. The almost empty bottle of liqueur had a lot to answer for.

Including the words *Not pregnant. Not living with a guy. Not in a relationship* flipping and twisting inside her head.

"You know what my problem is?" Sable asked, expecting no one to answer.

"Where do you want to start?" That from her mother.

Bear shot Mercy a look and she held her hands up in surrender. Then he looked back at Sable and said, "Tell me."

"I go about things all backwards."

"What things?"

"My career, for one. I started out on a high—gallery show, prize money, fame—and only then did I have to work like crazy to earn a reputation."

"Right."

"And then, there's…the other thing. If you love someone, you don't ask them to have your baby first. You ask them if they'll have you."

The one time she would have liked for her mother to perk up with a sharp comment, Mercy remained all too quiet.

Sable licked her dry lips. Leaned towards Bear and, voice low, said, "But I couldn't do that. Because I didn't come back here for him."

"Please." *Now* her mother perked up.

While Bear said, "But you just said you loved him."

"What? No, I didn't!"

"Yeah, you did," said Carleen, most helpfully.

Bear gave her a soft smile. "You said, and

I quote, 'If you love someone, you don't ask them—'"

Sable flapped a hand at Bear till he stopped talking. Till the café was deadly quiet.

"She did," said Mercy, "didn't she?"

Sable's breaths were suddenly hard to come by.

"Sable," said Mercy, waiting for her daughter to look her way. "Answer me this: if you had to choose, right now, would you pick Rafe, or Rafe's child?"

Bear sucked in an audible breath and held it. Mercy looked so hard into Sable's eyes there was no hope of faffing her way out of the question. While Carleen began singing "Stand By Your Man" under her breath in what amounted to a gorgeous singing voice.

Sable's voice shook as she said, "You told me my whole life *never* to believe a man is more important than my dreams."

"No," said Mercy, pointing a finger Sable's way. "I told you to figure out what those dreams are, before you even think about finding yourself a man. Unfortunately we had to move in next to Rafe Ruddy Thorne. And that was it. One look and you were a goner."

A muscle car revved its engine as it ambled

slowly down the street, the noise shaking the windows.

Rafe, Sable thought, her heart now thundering so loudly she could barely hear herself think. *Rafe* had been her dream. Wanting a child, a backyard, a home, that had all come later, when she'd begun believing that life might actually be possible, with him.

And yet she'd pushed him away.

So as not to hurt him. Because she thought he was better off without her. When she hadn't stopped to ask what *he* wanted. What he now thought was possible.

"Quick, I need Janie's number."

"Why? What are you going to do?"

"Really? You want me to say it out loud? Fine. I'm going to enlist her help in doing whatever it takes to show Rafe how much I love him. And want to be with him. For ever and ever. If he'll still have me."

"Hallelujah." That was Bear, his voice hitching with emotion.

A beat later, maybe two, Mercy sighed. Then she called out Janie's mobile number by heart.

Thank you, Sable mouthed as she held her phone to her ear.

Sable gave her mother a big kiss on the cheek,

before she waved to Bear, who was swiping a tear from his cheek, and bolted out of the door.

It took Janie another hour to open The Barn, move some exorbitantly expensive vehicles, find the keys to the VW and drive into town, giving Sable time to drink copious amount of water.

She sat in the passenger seat, running a hand over the dimpled dash, the old junkyard seats, wondering how she hadn't realised—seeing it kept under a protective cloth next to Ferraris and Lamborghinis and Mustangs that were near priceless in value—how precious it was to him.

Because *she* was precious to him. Even after what she'd done. Even after how she'd left. He'd held a flame for her. And he'd forgiven her.

Only now she realised, she had never forgiven herself.

It explained why she'd let herself fall into such one-sided relationships. Why she'd convinced herself Rafe was better off without her. Why she'd been so ready to push him away at the first hurdle.

Because she loved him so much she only wanted the very best for him.

Never stopping to wonder if she might be the best for him!

She wasn't perfect. Mistakes would be made. Differences navigated. Disagreements hashed out. And bad things might happen, to them and theirs.

But she loved Rafe. Deeply, wholly, ferociously. So much it expanded to encompass the people around her. Bear and Stan and Janie and this town. This beautiful, charming, crazy little town.

They hit Laurel Avenue, right as one of the McGlinty boys was cordoning it off, sending any traffic on a detour. A detour away from Rafe.

Sable wound down the ancient window. *Squeak-squeak-squeak.* "Fred? Ed? Let us through!"

"Can't, Ms Sutton. Mumma said we need to start putting out the cones for her parade."

Squeak-squeak-squeak. Janie wound down her window too. "The parade is *tomorrow* afternoon, you goose!"

Fred—or was it Ed?—blanched. "But Mumma—"

"Let 'em through!" Carleen and Mercy stood outside Bear's, holding one another up.

"Thanks, Carleen!" called Sable.

Carleen lifted a fresh bottle of Pumpkin Spice liqueur in salute.

Janie shot Sable a grin. "What happens during

the Pumpkin Spice Festival stays— Nah, who am I kidding? Whatever happens today will go down in town folklore for ever."

The McGlinty boy hopped to it, moving traffic cones so that the VW could sneak through. And they were off once more. Heading towards the Radiance Reserve.

It was stop start traffic as they hit the path leading into Reserve. Over the tops of the trees Sable could see the tip of the Ferris wheel turning over, and she thought she could even hear the fairground music. And where the day before there had been acres of fresh green grass, there was now row upon row of sleek European sports cars that would look more at home in Monte Carlo, along with dented old Datsuns with their owners shining them up with pride, and more FJ Holdens than she could count.

Spying a gap in the low wooden fence lining the path, Janie hooked left, bumped over the small gutter and hit the grass.

Gripping the window frame, Sable said, "Do you know where you're going?"

"Yep," Janie insisted, eyes scanning the crowd as she bumped over the grassy ground. "I helped create the mud map for every car coming today. Rafe has me on the payroll as Bossy Little Sister."

Someone official-looking suddenly jumped in their way, holding a glowing arrow. Waving madly that they head off to the left. Janie rolled her eyes, but did as she was told, and they soon found themselves in a sea of Beetles and Kombi vans, all splashed in bright, hippy colours and motifs.

Janie parked, and they both hopped out of the car.

Sable strained to see Rafe through the streams of cars and the burgeoning crowd. It would be like finding a needle in a haystack. Standing on tiptoes made no difference. But what if…?

She walked around the car, pressed her hands into the bonnet. "Think it'll hold me?"

Janie grinned. "Never know till you try."

Sable kneed her way up onto the bonnet, pausing for a second when it made a light crumpling sound. If the thing buckled, she did know someone who could fix it.

She redistributed her weight and slowly stood atop the curved roof of the old Beetle. And wondered what the hell she'd been thinking.

Rafe. She was thinking about Rafe.

Eagle eyes on high alert she scanned the crowd.

Looking for dark curls. Broad shoulders. Sending out sensory feelers for a man of strength and goodness. A great big beautiful forgiving heart. And hotness that surpassed all hotness.

There! By the big rigs. Dark chambray shirt and jeans while everyone around him was rugged up in scarves and beanies. All that glorious inner heat keeping him toasty warm.

Sable shivered, wrapping the leather jacket around her T-shirt. Wishing she could wrap herself around him. Hoping, if she hadn't screwed everything up so badly in her effort to do right, she might yet get that chance.

He was distracted, phone to his ear. Other hand on his hip. Frowning off into the distance.

Sable's next breath in was a shaky one.

"Hey!" called Janie from way down below.

Sable didn't dare look. She couldn't take her eyes off Rafe lest she lose him. Again.

"I found her! She's here! With the Kombi vans."

"You talking to Rafe?" Sable asked.

Janie gave her a thumbs-up.

In the distance, Rafe spun on his heel, his gaze glancing off the cars in between them and the growing groups of people who were now turned her way, pointing at the crazy lady standing atop the car, as if expecting some kind of announcement. Or catastrophe.

Rafe's hand flew out to the side as he shrugged. Sable imagined she could see his frown deepening. Oh, how she loved that brooding frown. Proof how seriously he took himself, and his place in the world. How deeply the man felt.

"Tell him to look up," Sable said.

"Look up!" said Janie.

Rafe did just that. Stilling the moment his eyes found hers.

"Give me the phone," Sable said, carefully crouching down and holding out her hand.

Janie reached up and slapped the mobile into her palm.

The phone was warm when it reached her ear. Or maybe her ear was warm already. She felt hot all over. Feverish. But determined.

She had no plan of what she ought to say. In fact her entire future felt blank. Beautifully so. No plans, wants, wishes, dreams, hopes, regrets or fears bar what she might do in the next minute. Bar convincing Rafe to give her another chance.

"Rafe," she said into the phone, her voice little more than a breath.

His voice came to her, deep and dubious. "I thought you'd gone."

"Still here. Can we talk?"

"Kinda busy right now."

Sable blinked and the hundreds of cars still streaming into the park came back into focus.

"Right. Of course," she said. "Yeah. Me too."

His laughter came through the phone all tinny and faraway. But she could feel him thinking. Considering. Weighing up what was more important.

And the sense that she had pulled away, right to the very outer reaches of the invisible rubber band that had always held them together, softened, just a little.

"What the hell are you doing on top of the car, Sutton?"

"Not just any car. My car. The one you made me. With your own bare hands. Because you were smitten with me. Even back then. Even when you kept telling yourself you couldn't be. When you were so convinced you—that wild Thorne kid—didn't know how to be happy."

"Sable—"

"I had to see you and it felt like the quickest way."

She heard him breathe in deep. Saw him, even

at a distance, do the same. Then his head dropped, his hand went back to his hip.

She waited. The whole world waited. Trapped between breaths. Between heartbeats. Then he lifted his head.

"Sable," he said, only this time his voice was a rough, sexy, surrender.

The urge to go to him, Hollywood style, leaping from car rooftop to car rooftop, was huge.

"Don't even think about it," he said, his voice a low growl.

She felt it in her spine. Her veins. The tips of every hair on her body.

She teetered but stayed upright. "You can't possibly know what I'm thinking."

"I can. And I do."

Yeah, she thought, doing a little of her own deep breathing. He really could. He really did.

Her heart trembled, her knees shook, as she said, "So what am I thinking?"

He ran a hand over his mouth. Then looked at her. Right at her. She felt it, like an arrow through the heart, even from so far away. "You're thinking that maybe you were a little hasty yesterday, pulling the rug out from under us."

"Really? What else?"

"You're thinking you didn't give my plan, my request, proper consideration."

Sable sighed. "Then tell me. Tell me what you think I should do."

"Stay," he said as he took off, his long legs eating up the ground between them. "Don't move."

"But you're busy."

"Story of my life. Though clearly that word takes on less meaning when you're in the picture."

"You're welcome?"

Another laugh. Another skitter of sensation down her spine. This one scattered all the way to the ends of her fingers and toes. She shuffled her feet a little wider in case her knees gave way, only to feel the roof of the car strain.

She wobbled. Then the car wobbled back. Her foot slipping an inch.

"Rafe?"

He must have heard the panic in her voice as he began to run. Towards her. In slow motion.

Well, not in slow motion, but that was how it felt. As if he were now the one pulling out the Hollywood stops. Only she couldn't run towards him too, as she was stuck on top of a car, in slippery city-girl boots.

One wrong move and the car would go full Herbie and send her flying.

And then there he was in all his dark-curled, broad-shouldered, unshaven glory. His perma-frown in place, the phone still at his ear.

She made to crouch, to go to him, only to be met with a creak. And a groan. The ground seemed to swell and keel. And it suddenly felt a longer way down than it had been up.

She froze, knees bent, one hand out to balance, the other holding Janie's phone to her ear.

"Sable," Rafe's voice murmured in her ear a split second before she heard it in person.

"Hi," she said into the phone, to him.

"Everything okay up there?"

"Yep. I'm fine."

"Meaning you're in straight-out panic mode, right?"

"Mmm-hmm."

He put his phone in his back pocket and held out a hand.

She tossed him Janie's phone. He looked at it, passed it on to his sister and gave her a look that sent her off in the direction from whence he'd come. Chatting to the car owners, directing, taking over. Bossy Little Sister in action.

Rafe climbed onto the car as if it were nothing.

A mountain goat. Or a man who knew his way around the load-bearing walls of a car chassis.

When he reached the roof he took her around the waist and drew her to her knees, then her backside. Weight distributed over the windscreen frame, she sat, legs sliding down the window. While he uncurled his long self beside her.

"I thought you'd gone," he said, looking down at his hands, playing with a blade of grass he must have nabbed along the way.

The constant movement of his hands was so familiar, she near choked on the feelings spilling through her. "I thought about it."

"Couldn't get a bus ticket?" he asked, glancing her way.

She nodded. Slowly. Mesmerised by the emotion in his eyes. The heat. The hope.

That hope was everything. Her touchstone. Her true north. The hope that she'd finally, truly found her way back to him.

It was enough for Sable to stop prevaricating and leap. Figuratively. For she was clutching every muscle in case the entire car deflated underneath them.

"Rafe." She swallowed. Watched his dark gaze follow the small movements in her face. "When you asked me to stay the night of the dinner party, I know you said you wanted it to be a 'no-strings' thing, but the thing is…"

She dragged her eyes from his before she found herself lost in his eyes. "The thing is, I've spent so much of my life on the run. First with Mercy, dragging me from town to town. Then from my own shadow as I struggled to figure out where I fit every time we stopped. Then you came along and for the first time in my life I knew what it meant to stand still. To simply be. It was a heady thing. Magical really. Overwhelming. So much so I ran from you too."

She glanced up at Rafe to find his eyes on her. Gaze full, dark with emotion. Then his hand slid slowly around her back, hooked her around the middle and drew her in. His chin landing on top of her downcast head.

It was so sweet, so tender, her throat threatened to close up. But she had more to say.

"I came here with a plan," she said. "But a little voice kept telling me that it was an excuse. That I was still running away. From LA, sure, all those opinions of people I'd never met. But mostly from the anger I felt at myself for all those lost years. And when I found out, yesterday, that I wasn't pregnant, it felt like a slap from the universe."

Sable scratched at a loose thread in Rafe's jeans. Before her hand landed on his knee. He took her fingers in his, turned them over, entwined them together.

"I promise you weren't the only one."

She slid her head out from under his, shook her hair from her face and looked back at him.

"I was caught up in the romance of it all. Your return, the feelings still between us, the notion of a ready-made family. When you told me it didn't take... I'm so sorry, Sable."

He lifted his hand, ran his thumb along her cheek, gathering a tear she hadn't even felt drop.

"Do you know how rare it is to fall the first time you try?" she asked.

"I'm thinking, pretty rare."

"Even the healthiest people in the healthiest relationships can struggle. So much comes down to luck and timing."

"I can imagine."

"And..." She stopped. Swallowed. "And the thing is, I don't want to stop trying. With you. For as long as you'll let me. And if it never takes, if it's not meant to be, then...we can find another way. Or not. We can take it as it comes. I can handle that. I can handle anything, so long as we do it together. For the truth is, in coming back here I was running. But I was always running back to you."

Then there was nothing—no colour, no sound, no people, no light, not one thing in the entire universe bar Rafe. The glint in his dark eyes. The way his fingers gripped hers. The way his eyes drank her in, as if he couldn't quite believe she was real.

He lifted his hand, this time sliding it behind her neck, cupping her, owning her. His words were a blur amongst the sensations taking her over at his nearness, his touch, the rumble of his voice, the heat of him. "Then *stay*, Sutton. *Be with me.* No rules, no promises, no transactions. Because you want to. And because you know that I want you to, too. Stay. For ever."

Sable threw herself into Rafe's arms. He rocked back as he caught her, the car rocking beneath them too. Sable scrambled to find purchase, the heels of her boots scraping against the windscreen.

"I've got you," Rafe murmured into her hair. "I've got you."

And the words hit so deep, she could have sobbed till she was nothing but a husk.

"Well, I've got you too," she said when she could finally find her words. Holding onto his shoulders, she leaned back. Heart fierce, throat tight, filled with such certainty she barely recognised herself. And yet felt more fully herself than she had in years.

"I love you, Rafe," she said, the words she'd held back for fear she'd made it impossible to ever hear them back falling from her lips with ease. "I always have. Being away from you, I was only ever half of myself. And I thought that was enough. But now... I'm back. And I love you. And it's everything. No matter our luck. No matter our timing. No matter where we live. No matter if we are blessed with a baby. Or not."

When she stopped to take a breath, Rafe pressed her hair away from her face, and held her cheeks and looked deep into her eyes. His voice gruff as he said, "Ditto."

Man of few words, her guy, but the words he said, he meant.

She pressed forward and kissed him. Lips to lips. Eyes slammed shut. A promise. And a thank you. Everything she felt releasing on a rush of breath. A rush of realisation. Of admitting something she'd always known.

He pulled back. Said, "I wasn't done."

"Oh. Right. What else is there to say?"

Rafe laughed, the move lighting up his whole

face. "Just that I love you too. Loved you since the first moment I saw you. Loved you more every day you let me near. I loved you when I first kissed you. Loved you even when it pained me to give you time—to grow up, to be sure that you really wanted a lug like me. I loved you as you glared at people who dared hold their bags tighter when I walked by. When you stood up for me against my father. When you took to Janie like a sister. I loved you even as I lost you. Twice."

Sable felt the tear fall that time. And the next. For she'd been more than forgiven. She'd been seen. Understood. And given the space to figure out what Rafe had known from day one.

That she was his and he was hers and they were more together than they could ever be apart.

Sable was ready, aching, by the time his lips met hers.

It was a slow-burn kind of kiss. The kind that lit a fuse, trickling deep, burning heat through every part of her until she was alight. Melting. Desperate for the heat to be quenched.

She threw her leg over his, gripped his glorious hair, moaned into his mouth—

A cheer woke her from the dream, to find it wasn't a dream.

Sable's eyes snapped open to find herself sitting on top of a dented black VW, in the small alpine town of Radiance, Victoria, surrounded by strangers—cheering strangers—and classic cars as far as the eye could see. The scent of wet leaves and damp dirt and petrol filled the air. The scent of home.

"We have an audience," she murmured.

Rafe glanced out over the crowd, looking far less discombobulated than she felt. Until he ran a hand through his hair, a shaky hand. Big, strong and in demand, he was a quiet small-town boy at heart. One who needed few and loved fiercely. It made her smile.

Till he said, "You stood on top of a car, waving me down like an idiot. What did you think would happen?"

She thumped him on the arm. Then flapped her hand towards the crowd. "I didn't think *that* would happen."

Only it didn't make her stomach churn the way it had when people stared at her in LA. Or when she walked through town. Because she *knew* she had nothing to be ashamed of.

Then, seeing his gaze was on her mouth, hungry and intense, she sank back into another kiss. A warm kiss. Lingering. Full of promise. And forgiveness. And lots of lovely, fresh, blooming new feelings.

People cheered a little more, clapping and cat-calling, before they eventually moved on. The cars beckoning their attention.

"You taste like cinnamon," Rafe said eons later.

"And cloves," said Sable, in between kisses she now rained over his cheeks, his jaw, his neck. "And pepper. And pumpkin. And vodka."

He shook his head. "Ah, Pumpkin Festival. You do bring out the crazy."

Right on cue, a cheer split the air. Sable tipped her head to follow the sound. A tunnel of people in the Mustang aisle whooped and clapped. And between them came flashes of bare skin as Carleen McGlinty ran stark naked through the crowd.

"No two guesses as to who else has been into the vodka," said Rafe on a laugh, pulling her deeper into his arms.

Sable grinned. Lifted her other leg to drape it over Rafe's. And settled in. The groans and creaks of the metal no longer a concern.

If this car fell apart, they had others. One of the benefits of being with a brilliant car restorer.

Feeling as light as air, Sable breathed in the

colour all around her. The lush green of the grass, the purple of the mountain peeking out over the bursts of oranges and reds and rich autumnal brown of the trees. Above it all the sky—light and bright, a soft velvety blue peppered with tufts of fluffy white clouds.

And then there was Rafe, the hot, dark, solid presence beside her.

Smiling, with every inch of her body, she breathed out fully, and closed her eyes.

Feeling safe, and happy, and home.

EPILOGUE

SABLE STEPPED OUT through the front door of The Barn, tucked her light summer wrap around her nightie, and curled her toes into the warm wood of the new deck beneath her feet.

The sky above was a clear blue dome. Mount Splendour covered in the green of fresh spring growth. The air was cool but by midday it would be scorching.

Sensing movement, Sable found Rafe standing over a pile of dried wood, T-shirt dripping in sweat as he chopped the logs for next winter. The new fireplaces they'd put in the lounge and the sitting room when they'd converted The Barn into a home were possibly her favourite additions.

Well, that and the nursery.

Feet bare, she padded over the lush green grass outside their back door. As often happened when she came within touching distance of Rafe, she felt the world shimmer around her.

She reached for him, wrapping her arms around his waist, laying a kiss on his shoulder, tucking her head into the warmth of his back. A vision flashed inside her head, a memory of another such moment, or a wish she'd once had. Then it was gone. Reality being so much better.

And the air kept on shimmering, with the warm buzz of coming summer.

"Good morning." Rafe's voice hummed through his back into her ear.

"Isn't it?"

"Eaten yet?"

"I just woke up. What time is it?"

"Does it matter?"

Sable smiled, and felt it blossom through her. "Not a jot."

Rafe was in town for a few days, with a big old Cadillac to keep him busy and a wife who had plans to keep him busier again. Mercy and Stan would be coming over for lunch, but not for a few hours yet.

"You looked too peaceful all tucked up in bed," said Rafe. "Snoring away."

"I don't snore."

"You didn't snore. Since munchkin came on the scene, it's another story."

Sable glared at him as she tried to see if he was kidding. Then—

"Oh!" she said, her hand moving to her growing belly.

"Sutton?" Rafe spun to face her. Throwing the axe aside. Dark eyes worried, before his gaze dropped to her hand. "What's wrong?"

"I keep telling you, don't call me Sutton. It's Thorne now."

"Hell, woman, you're as bad as your mother."

She went to glare at him when… "There!" she said, grabbing his hand and laying it under hers. "Wait for it."

She felt it again. Like bubbles popping.

Rafe's eyebrow kicked north. "You snore. And now you have gas. If I'd known this was how things were going to be—"

"Shush, you big doofus. It's a kick. Those bubbly feelings, that's the baby kicking."

Rafe's eyes grew comically wide, before his gaze dropped once more to her belly. Then he dropped to his knees, jeans sinking into the dewy ground. His hand moving a little to the left so he could rest his ear against her belly. His other hand wrapped around her wrist, the one sporting her arrow bracelet, his thumb running over the thin charm.

They stood there, the morning sun filtering over them, their land beneath their feet, pollen floating on the warm air, birdsong wafting to them from the copse of trees giving them privacy from Janie's Airstream—

Bubbles! One after the other.

Their eyes met. And they laughed as one.

Before Rafe pressed to his feet, and kissed her long and hard. Basking in the surety that their baby, their little girl—or boy—was happily, healthily moving around inside Sable's womb.

For all their big plans it had taken them a full year to fall pregnant.

Which was, actually, pretty perfect. As it had given them a whole year to find their new normal.

Sable liked to sleep in—heading out into the wilderness in the afternoon light, to find angles and damage and regrowth to photograph.

Rafe was up before the birds, answering correspondence from all over the world as his reputation grew and opportunities bloomed. When he travelled in search of cars that needed tending, needed care, it was with alacrity, making time to check in several times a day. Sable liked him checking in.

And together they'd converted The Barn into

a warm, spacious, two-storey space, filled with homey rugs and plush furniture.

There was an art studio bathed in natural light, and a five-car garage in which to keep Rafe's most precious cars, and one VW Beetle— newly panel-beaten, freshly painted in a deep rich glossy black. They'd kept the stairs leading to the loft.

"You know that envelope the doctor gave us?"

Rafe didn't have to ask which one. He drew himself back to his feet, a hand still on her belly. "What about it?"

"I reckon we should open it."

Rafe had wanted to know the gender, Sable had not. Having witnessed such impasses many times over, the doctor had gently suggested writing down the answer and popping it in an envelope. Just in case.

But here, now, with Rafe holding her with such tenderness, such strength and solidity, Sable knew she would give him anything he ever wanted. No questions asked. No strings.

"Are you sure?" he asked, dark eyes gleaming with such hope it made her laugh. "Because I can wait."

"Come on." Sable took him by the hand and led him back towards the house.

The envelope was currently attached to their fridge with a magnet Mercy had made. Sable's mother was trying out all kinds of creative endeavours these days. Sketching. Ceramics. Silversmithing. It was odd. But lovely. Softening. But if the baby ever called her anything but Mercy, there'd be hell to pay.

Sable took the envelope from the fridge and handed it to Rafe. "You do the honours."

Breathing deep, his big chest rising and falling with emotion, Rafe gently tore the lip of the sealed paper.

"So," Sable said, "if it's a girl, Mercy, if it's a boy, Stan?"

"Not for all the oil in the Middle East."

"Carleen or Bear?"

Rafe shot her a look that made her knees go weak.

Sable grinned and said, *"Fine."*

"I don't trust that word a jot."

"Mmm. Smart man. You ready for this?"

"Hell, yeah. But are you?"

"More than ready."

She leaned over and placed a kiss on Rafe's beautiful mouth. The kiss deepened near as soon as it began. She hooked her fingers into the front of his sweaty T-shirt, the scent of him, the taste of him, filling her senses until she was drunk with it.

Rafe groaned as he pulled her into him.

In the back of her mind Sable heard the sound of paper hitting the floor. The envelope. The news inside it unread.

The baby's gender... They'd get to that.

They had time.

All the time in the world.

* * * * *